ACROSS THE BRIDGE TO CHINA

Also by Gwenn Boardman Petersen

Living in Singapore

ACROSS THE BRIDGE TO CHINA

by

GWENN BOARDMAN PETERSEN

ELSEVIER/NELSON BOOKS
New York

Library of Congress Cataloging in Publication Data

Petersen, Gwenn Boardman.
  Across the bridge to China.

  Includes index.
    1. China—Description and travel—1976–
2. Petersen, Gwenn Boardman. I. Title.
DS712.P47 1979   915.1′04′5   79–4171
ISBN 0–525–66622–2

Published in the United States by Elsevier/Nelson Books, a division of Elsevier-Dutton Publishing Company, Inc., New York. Published simultaneously in Don Mills, Ontario, by Thomas Nelson and Sons (Canada) Limited.

Printed in the U.S.A.   First Edition
10 9 8 7 6 5 4 3 2 1

CONTENTS

	A Note on Chinese Words	7
	Building a Bridge	9
1.	The View from Hong Kong	17
2.	Family Ties	34
3.	The Streets of Canton	48
4.	Sunday in the Park	68
5.	Abacus, Brush, and *Little Red Book*	89
6.	Soldier, Shipbuilder, Statistician	114
7.	Two-Way Mirror	139
8.	Commune Living	162
9.	My Father's Country	179
10.	Up from Slavery	200
11.	Afterthoughts	222
	Index	237

A NOTE ON CHINESE WORDS

THOUGH CHINESE words and proper names have been kept to a minimum in this book, readers may sometimes find the variant spellings confusing. The system of romanization used by the People's Republic of China (*pinyin*) writes the city of Peking as *Beijing*. Most Westerners, including Chinese-Americans, are more familiar with the Wade-Giles system. So it takes them quite a while to recognize Kwangchow (Canton) as Guangzhou, and to realize that the familiar Chung Kuo (Middle Kingdom) is now Zhong Guo.

The Peking version, however, gives a much more accurate rendering of the Chinese sounds. The sound that the Wade-Giles system gives as *cho,* for instance, should be sounded as *j.* The letter *p,* as in Peking, is pronounced as *b.* Chinese maps show Yuehsiu Park in Canton as Yuexiu, and Chenhai Tower becomes Zhenhai. But the Chinese themselves usually bow to common foreign usage in rendering Mao Tse-tung's name as in the Wade-Giles system, although the *ts* is really pronounced *dz,* and Tsetung is usually written as one word.

7

ACROSS THE BRIDGE TO CHINA

BUILDING
A BRIDGE

THE PEOPLE'S REPUBLIC OF
CHINA. Is it a clean, crime-free paradise? Do all the workers sing in the fields or dance down in the coal mines? Is
there anyone who is *not* a part-time painter of cabbages or
a poet singing the praises of Iron Girls drilling for oil?

Or is the PRC a hell in which Mass Man (or Woman)
must move in lockstep from the first 5 A.M. breath of outdoor exercises to an evening recitation of Little Red Truths
memorized from the pages of the late Chairman Mao?

For thousands of young Americans with family ties to
China, trying to get answers to these questions is particularly frustrating. Even those with relatives in Canton—less
than two hundred kilometers from Hong Kong by train—
sometimes feel as though their cousins lived as far away as
China's distant borders in the Himalayas or deep in the
Mongolian wastes.

Many want desperately to be part of the New China—
and they cannot understand why their own requests to visit

Kwangtung Province remain unanswered, whereas wealthy passengers aboard cruise ships can take three-day excursions into Canton and Shanghai as easily as most of us can spend a weekend at the beach.

Sometimes, even before the diplomatic thaw that followed the Ping-Pong matches and President Nixon's visit at the beginning of the 1970's, it was easier to visit China if one had family there. Yet even here, a combination of bureaucratic whimsy and simple luck permitted one cousin to get into China less than six months after the first inquiry, while another might be desperately writing letters to Peking three years later, without getting a reply.

A few were driven to brief—and illegal—identity switches, taking advantage of a system that permitted Hong Kong and Macao residents to visit their Kwangtung hometowns by showing an ID card at the border. Others traveled to Hong Kong only to find that they could not sneak in, and they got no closer to Kwangtung Province than the view from a hilltop provided by afternoon tours out of downtown Kowloon hotels.

For most Chinese-Americans, during the years when diplomatic ties between China and the United States were broken (following United States support of Chiang Kai-shek's regime on Taiwan), the land of their ancestors was as remote and exotic as it had seemed to Europeans reading Pegolotti's fourteenth-century account of *The Safe Road to Peking*. New ethnic-studies courses, TV specials, and ever-multiplying travelers' tales of "friendship groups" whetted their appetites. . . . In the past two or three years a visit to China has been changing from dream to reality, as more and more visitors are allowed in.

Cultural taboos and inhibitions still prevent many of the visitors from speaking out in their own voices, lest they embarrass Chinese relatives or break the family tradition that discourages plain speaking and forbids the exposure of "family matters" to outsiders.

In this book, "Joe" and "Eileen" try to speak out for all those Chinese-Americans who have been lucky enough to see life inside the People's Republic of China for themselves. They have not found clear answers to the Chinese puzzles—although they are convinced that the truth lies somewhere between the extremes of pro-Taiwan hostility and the enthusiasms of American tourist-converts.

The photographs illustrating the following pages were not taken by Joe and his friends. To avoid possible embarrassment for their families, I should like to make it plain that, although the narrative and attitude are Joe's, all of the illustrations are the result of my own brief visit to Canton and Kwangtung Province in 1978. And of course none of the residents of the People's Republic of China who appear in these pictures should be identified either with the families of visiting Chinese-Americans or with the various conversations quoted.

My freedom to move about the streets of Canton, to wander about and to take photographs during the hours not scheduled for special activities gave me opportunities to meet the Chinese people. I was not accompanied by an interpreter during these wanderings, and if any errors have occurred in captioning, I hope that my kind friends will forgive me.

I should like to take this opportunity to thank them all for their courtesy and their kindness. Communication was not easy. Many people in Canton do not speak English, and my knowledge of Chinese is very limited.

Joe's experiences often seemed to have provided the captions for these photos: the young couple walking hand-in-hand (but taking it for granted that they would not marry until the approved age); families enjoying the beauties of their parks, even in the rain; the evident pleasure of factory and farm workers who had come directly from their jobs to front-row seats for a performance by Kwangchow's acrobats. Whatever their private sorrows—or their private feelings about a committee-regulated life—they were without exception the most happy-looking and seemingly contented people I have ever met in my travels.

Sometimes, the surface of the rural picture did not appear to have changed in a hundred years. The simple village homes—often with the only daytime illumination coming through the open door of windowless rooms—are unbelievably bare by Western standards. But in comparison with what I have heard of village life forty years ago, the families are prosperous.

I was in the People's Republic of China a few days after the Fifth National Party Congress, when changes in the Constitution and various new policies were being announced. Wages are to be increased, overtime pay restored, college entrance exams and special professional schools reinstated. Chairman Hua was even using the words of a famous Mao Tse-tung quotation: "Let a hundred flowers blossom, let a hundred schools of thought contend."

In December, 1978, President Carter and Chairman Hua Kuo-feng announced full diplomatic relations between the United States and the People's Republic of China. One month later, Vice-Premier Teng Hsiao-ping arrived in Washington for talks with American government and business leaders. At the same time, the magazine *China Reconstructs* (published in Peking for overseas readers, in English, French, Spanish, Arabic, and German) gave further evidence of new trends as "all over China eyes are turned towards modernization." In speaking of their program of "four modernizations" the Chinese still quote the words and ideas of Chairman Mao Tse-tung and Premier Chou

En-lai. Yet every day brings new announcements of radical changes in education, a revival of interest in classical art and literature, fewer political meetings, more overseas contacts, and even "the restoration of rights, jobs, and private property to former capitalists." Small signs of change even appear in the retelling of ancient legends (including the tale of the mythical beasts who gave Canton the name of "City of Rams"), in the publication of a real-life Chinese love story, and in cartoons that poke gentle fun at minor party officials.

Yet it is too soon to tell if the changes suggested by constitutional revisions, official speeches, and new slogans will really change the scene that Joe and his friends observed. Even the radical changes of the 1966 Cultural Revolution were not permanent. The "new" ideas of 1978 may well be discarded by the 1980's, the rural scene may well appear as unchanged in another century as it seemed to visitors in the spring of 1978.

Joe's adventure began in Hong Kong. . . .

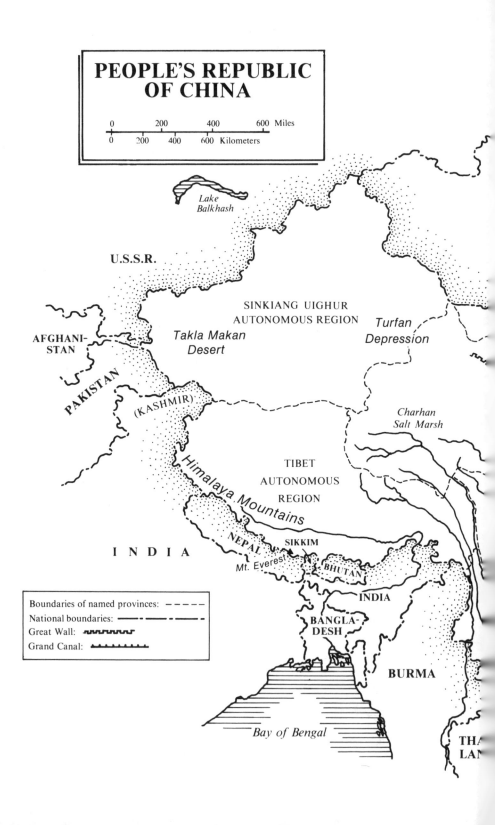

PEOPLE'S REPUBLIC OF CHINA

| 0 | 200 | 400 | 600 | Miles |
| 0 | 200 | 400 | 600 | Kilometers |

Lake
Balkhash

U.S.S.R.

SINKIANG UIGHUR
AUTONOMOUS REGION

Turfan
Depression

AFGHANI-
STAN

Takla Makan
Desert

PAKISTAN

(KASHMIR)

Charhan
Salt Marsh

Himalaya Mountains

TIBET
AUTONOMOUS
REGION

I N D I A

NEPAL

SIKKIM

Mt. Everest

BHUTAN

INDIA

Boundaries of named provinces: – – – – –
National boundaries: ——-—-——--
Great Wall: ᴨᴨᴨᴨᴨᴨᴨᴨ
Grand Canal: ▲▲▲▲▲▲▲▲

BANGLA-
DESH

BURMA

Bay of Bengal

THA
LA

1

THE VIEW FROM HONG KONG

THE CHINESE MAINLAND stretches beyond the horizon: home for about 900 million people, a land that covers 9.6 million square kilometers—tropical islands with coconuts and coral, deserts of colored sand, the world's highest mountain, and the deep Turfan Depression. I have read that close to half the world's population is Chinese, that China's Yangtze River alone drains an area in which live 10 percent of all the people on earth. But I seek only one city: Kwangchow—known in the West as Canton—the city of my father's birth.

Looking out of the plane's windows, I seek clues to the land of my ancestors. And I am disappointed. The harbor looks much like New York or Hamburg; the buildings could be in Detroit or Dallas. The over-water approach to Kai Tak Airport is reminiscent of the approach to San Francisco International. The only sign of the past is a huge junk putting out to sea, much like the vessels whose cargoes of spices lured Christopher Columbus in search of Cathay.

The plane wheels screech on the runway, and already we are on Chinese soil. For although Hong Kong, on the island across the bay, has been a British Crown Colony since 1843, the airport itself is on the mainland side. On this side of Victoria Harbor, the People's Republic of China is the landlord. Great Britain's ninety-nine-year lease on the New Territories runs out in 1997.

The Chinese mainland. Yet the streets are much like those back home in San Francisco's Chinatown. From the taxi window we can see grannies in their black jackets and trousers poking about among stacks of mushrooms and melons. Along Stockton Street at home I often see similar shopkeepers reaching into a tank to hook a nice carp for someone's supper, or handily wringing the neck of a white duck above a sidewalk crate.

Hotel check-in in Hong Kong has no distinctively Chinese qualities—only the sounds outside the window provide exciting hints of the "real" China, though I should have realized we were not much closer to the modern Chinese scene than a New Englander sitting down to a TV dinner of chicken chow mein.

This is the world that seems so romantic and so exotic to my Western friends: sounds of a flute, the clash of gong and cymbals, incense smoke drifting out of a temple doorway, strange shapes of sausage and pressed duck at a market stall.

It is only the surface of Hong Kong, and it is misleading. But Cousin Eileen had lived there for two years. She reminded me not to fall into "chop suey" thinking (my father's term for the attitude of anyone who goes out for a "Chinese" dinner and orders chop suey, an American invention).

Hong Kong is the place to get rid of some of the clichés before trying to come to terms with the land that has been

China's junks still sail the world's seas, just as they did when Marco Polo and Columbus sought the treasures of Cathay.

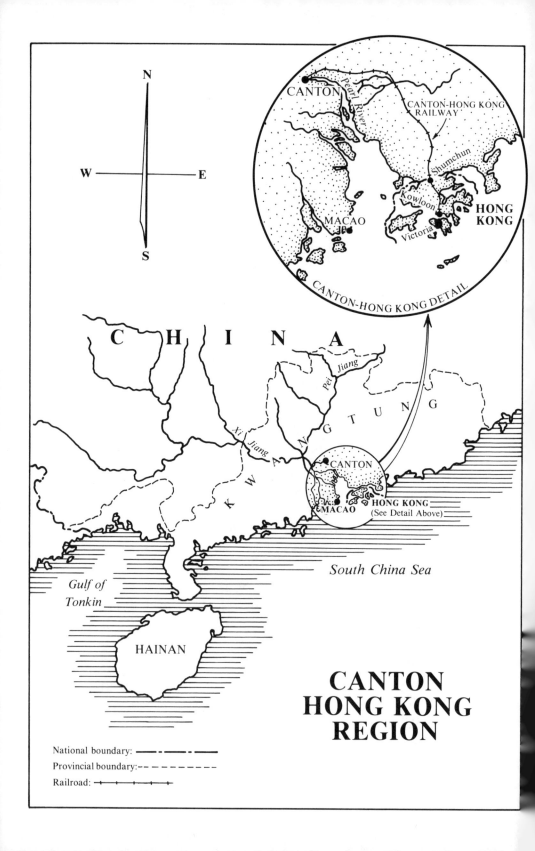

N

W   E

S

CANTON

Pearl River

CANTON-HONG KONG
RAILWAY

Shumchun

Kowloon

MACAO

Victoria

HONG
KONG

CANTON-HONG KONG DETAIL

C H I N A

Pei Jiang

K W A N G T U N G

Xi Jiang

CANTON

MACAO

HONG KONG
(See Detail Above)

South China Sea

Gulf of
Tonkin

HAINAN

CANTON
HONG KONG
REGION

National boundary: ▬ ▪ ▬ ▪ ▬

Provincial boundary: ▬ ▬ ▬ ▬ ▬

Railroad: ┼─┼─┼─┼─┼

so transformed from the country of my father's memories. In Hong Kong, 98 percent of the people are Chinese, and the majority (like the majority of California's Chinese community) have roots in the city of Canton or surrounding Kwangtung Province.

Here, in Hong Kong, everyone looks both ways—to the past and present, east and west. Families observe old traditions. They practice calligraphy and *wu shu* (the martial arts), they can quote Confucius and recite the words of the scholar-poets, whose first anthology was put together in 300 B.C.

At the same time, they look to the West: evenings of ballet and symphony; the recordings of rock stars; even porno movies. They are equally fluent in Cantonese and Oxford-accented English. And they coexist quite happily in the tourist world of Suzie Wong.

Six months in Shanghai and Peking had shown Eileen how far this is from the attitudes of the People's Republic of China!

We had only a few hours together. She was on her way back to Canada, and I did not want her to take away the excitement of making my own discoveries. So out we went to eat. . . .

Right away, I got a healthy reminder about the problems of communication in the PRC. I could not even sing for my supper. . . .

Strange that travelers returning from a two-week tour of China always claim to know so much about what goes on there. They never mention the biggest problem of all—not the unfamiliar ideas of Chinese communism, but the unfamiliar signs and sounds of the Chinese language itself.

How can anyone understand the complexities of Chinese life if they cannot even count as far as one, two, three? The ideographs of the written language can be read in

Hong Kong. Note the squatter's shacks on the hillside above the modern apartment buildings.

dozens of different ways. In common speech (*putonghua*) they count: *yi, er, san*. In Cantonese, it is *yut, yee, sahm*. That mundane vegetable, cabbage, is *bai tsai* in common speech. My mother calls it *bok choy*.

Although we often speak Cantonese at home, I soon discovered, when I asked for a snack of soup, dumplings, and cabbage, that I did not quite sing in tune. Chinese grammar is simple; what makes the language difficult are the various dialects, all spoken in different musical tones.

I had already begun with the humbling experience of feeling almost illiterate because I could read scarcely a hundred ideographs. Now, before the kindly restaurant proprietor, though he was patient as a first-grade teacher, I suffered dreadful moments of embarrassment as I confused my delightful mother with a pock-faced horse. (Depending on the tone you use, *ma* can be read as *mother, pockface, horse,* or *scold,* and the word sometimes just indicates the question: *Really?*)

Hardly arrived in Hong Kong, I was already beginning to wish that we had spoken Cantonese more often at home. In Canton later, I often felt like a crow among a field of nightingales, always croaking the wrong tune.

But as Eileen and I enjoyed our dumplings, I was already being reminded that, how ever well I might speak Chinese and how ever much I might look like other people on the streets of Canton, I would always look at the People's Republic of China with a kind of double vision: one eye thoroughly Western and the other clouded by old Chinese ideas.

Though we are linked by blood—we are second cousins—Eileen and I have different backgrounds. Her father was a professor in Hong Kong and is teaching in Canada now; mine works in a Bay Area auto plant. She was born in China, lived in Hong Kong, briefly attended an inter-

national school in Tokyo. Until now, I had never been outside California, except for a summer spent hitchhiking
through England and Europe. Her mother's Shanghai connections are rice-tub-fat merchants who managed to sur-
vive the old British rule as well as the Japanese occupation,
the labor riots and Kuomintang massacres, and, more recently, PRC political pressures. My family instead, apart
from one great-aunt who went off to Shanghai and an uncle
in Peking, stayed in Kwangtung Province until several of
them emigrated to the United States forty years ago.

We talked about the false romantic view some of our
American and Canadian friends have of Old China, the
China of mystery stories told by firelight, wicked landlords,
gorgeous soft-voiced girls. Our friends would not find it so
romantic if they also had to listen to my dad's voice of Old
Chinese authority, with his constant reminders: "Respect
your elders!" "Work hard." "Be careful with your money."
Whenever I wanted to leave my homework and go off to a
ball game, it was: "In China, we always studied harder."

And then there were the continual reminders from
other members of the family: "Mind what Auntie says." In
China, all older people, not just blood relatives, are "Uncle"
or "Auntie." When Eileen saw the film of mourning for the
late Premier in Peking, it seemed really strange to her to
hear mothers in the audience telling their children to "look
at Uncle Chou."

All our lives Eileen and I have been conditioned to
wonder, "What would the family say?" We are often both-
ered by the direct questions of our American friends and
often pretend to be calm or happy when our Western
friends don't mind showing that they are excited or sad.
Being familiar with the ideas of aunties gave us some clues
to some otherwise puzzling details of modern China, such
as the apparently de-sexed life-style of young people.

No Chinese-American is immune to his Chinese background, not even our swinging friend Jimmy back home. . . . He had shared a house with a Caucasian girl. His sister had married a young black lawyer. If he hadn't preferred *kung fu* to baseball, you would have taken him for a 100-percent California boy. Until he announced that he was going to get married, to a Chinese girl we scarcely knew and didn't like. Why on earth did he suddenly want to get married?

At his bachelor party, we got the answer: "It's a small thing to do for my father. He is nearly seventy now. I must give him a grandchild before he dies!" Since Jimmy likes to eat and his bride cannot even cook, he must believe in the old-fashioned concept—why else would he change his whole life-style?

In some ways Hong Kong, too, surprised us with its old-fashioned sights and sounds, its resemblance to our parents' memories. Yet it is really as much Western as Asian. Perhaps the only place in the world where that Old China still lingers is in Great Britain's leased land, the New Territories beyond Kowloon.

And so, as a first step to understanding modern China, I boarded the bus along with all the other foreign tourists. Listening to their chatter, I found—as Eileen had suggested I would—that the New Territories matched Western clichés and stereotypes, and hearing those false ideas restated helped me to change cultural gears before plunging into the modern People's Republic of China.

There were the "picturesque" Chinese of the travel brochures—boat people (*Tanka*), who spend their entire lives aboard junks. Yet in China proper the boat people, like those along the Pearl River in Canton, have been tidily rehoused in modern workers' villages. Beyond Kowloon, tourists click their shutters at the walled village of Kam

Tin, built by Cantonese immigrants about 500 years ago. The tourists are charmed by old ladies in black-fringed hats, the Hakka who turn shyly away from the cameras.

For me, the Hakka served as a reminder of Chinese prejudices. Hakka means "stranger"—although these people have lived in the area for a thousand years. All Western visitors will be strangers in China, even if they stay ten thousand days. How then could my hundred days in Canton be sufficient to restore old clan ties?

And then that emotional moment, when the bus stopped at the border. I climbed a hill, and there below lay my ancestral land.

To other tourists, it was no more than the bus driver's words: "Kwangtung Province, the rich country of the south, the major area for growing China's staple diet of rice and tea."

To me, it was a glimpse of home. There it lay, a misty black-ink scroll painting of Father's suddenly coming to life. Figures moving, dots in the landscape . . . almost deserted fields and houses . . . rice paddies . . . fish ponds.

What would it feel like to be down there, walking among the people?

Next morning, the idyllic feeling vanished, as I got my first taste of modern China's bureaucracy. For the official who handed over my visa was not a kindly father figure like the one who had welcomed Eileen. I was face-to-face with the counterpart of the stern woman I had read about who had quizzed visitors about their "terrible" life in the "bourgeois, capitalist" West.

There wasn't much time to worry about the possibility the Canton family would feel that way about me—just a few hours to shop for small gifts for the cousins, one last evening in the bright lights of the East-West city of Hong

The first glimpse of the People's Republic of China, from the Hong Kong side of the border.

Kong. Next morning an early start aboard the train bound for China.

In some ways, it was like the tourist bus—we even traveled beside the same road. But as I looked out through the windows now I realized that most Western visitors would always have this safe layer of glass—train, bus, hotel—between themselves and the Chinese scene, an interpreter always between them and the words and thoughts of the Chinese people.

Ready or not, *I* am going to be right in the picture, I said to myself.

The passengers seated around me—most of them Chinese—were thinning out. Children carried picnic lunches off at Sha Tin. Students got off the train at University Station, men and women went to market at Tai Po. Not many boarded, and at Sheung Shui everyone without papers for PRC entry was warned to get off the train.

How would it feel to live so close, and yet to be cut off from family in the PRC, as many still are? For those who did not like the political climate and had crossed over to Hong Kong, the narrow stream at the border station of Lo Wu is wider than the Pacific Ocean, though in fact it is narrower than the Carquinez Strait back in California. I cannot imagine how it would feel if the California tollgates were closed. How would my aunt in Sacramento feel if she could not hop on a bus whenever she wanted to and come down to San Francisco for a family supper or a friendly game of Mah-Jongg?

I began to have some doubts about what I would really see in China. So many of the reports I had heard sounded false. As an example, PRC officials claim that there is no betting on sporting events in China, no gambling. Yet apart from one friend who belongs to a stern religious group in southern California, I have never yet met a Chinese who does *not* gamble. That holds true just as much for fifth-generation business leaders in San Francisco and fresh-off-the boat kids newly arrived in Chinatown. Marco Polo noted more than seven hundred years ago that the Chinese were more addicted to gambling than any other people on earth. Even my most staid auntie loses her head just as soon as she hears the click of Mah-Jongg tiles. . . .

There was no more time for daydreaming. The scene from a magazine feature sprang to life: a real bridge indeed, covered, 275 meters long; double tracks down the middle, mail and wagonloads of goods passing freely. Yet for more than twenty years after the founding of the PRC in 1949, this bridge was a barrier as effective as the Great Wall once was in keeping out "barbarian" foreigners in the north.

Some of my ancestors looked down from the barricade of the Great Wall's granite, earth, and bricks more than 2,000 years ago. They had no desire to go beyond it, for China is the very center of the universe, its name still written with the characters Chung Kuo (Middle Country).

Zhōnghuá   Rénmín   Gònghéguó
(The People's Republic of China)

The characters for "China" are the first (Middle) and seventh (Country), reading from the left.

My heart should not have been thumping so fast. There is nothing to fear unless you are carrying an ounce of grass in or smuggling a gold ingot out. Treatment of foreigners in the twentieth century may have been unfriendly sometimes, but at least it has never been as radical as in the past—when 20,000 foreigners were killed in Hangchow in A.D. 875, or more recently, a group of Portuguese travelers, who had waited patiently to see the emperor for three years, were finally thrown into prison and died.

The other tourists on the train all seemed to be smiling. There was none of the tension and hostility of Berlin's Checkpoint Charlie. We were out of the train before I could worry any more about being classed as a "foreign devil" or a "big nose" because of my American passport.

It was time for my first lesson in modern Chinese thought. It doesn't matter whether you are the son of an immigrant Chinese laborer, a returning Shanghai business-

A group of foreign tourists arrive at Canton's modern railroad station.

man, or a member of one of those special groups carrying an official invitation. There is only one way to go into China: by walking.

For a moment, walking across that bridge seemed like a scene in one of those spy movies—the kind where prisoners are exchanged under the eyes of watchful uniformed guards. Will I make some dreadful error? Make a tactless comment on Chinese life? Perhaps never see California again?

No need to worry. The uniformed officials smiled as they stamped passports and checked papers. Tension was dispelled by the local equivalent of Musak—loudspeakers trying to soothe us with patriotic tunes. At the far end of the bridge, in fact, melodramatic fears seemed merely silly.

The scene is intensely normal—especially if you find scrubbed hospital waiting rooms, slipcovered chairs, and a smell of mothballs "normal." There are no reminders of

American railroads: no litter on the ground; no graffiti on walls or pillars; no slashed chairs—even the white covers are spotless. Everything seems antiseptic, it's so clean, even the air—apart from the noise pollution that eventually became a major irritant for me in the PRC.

It was my first sample of Big Brother life: music to march by, announcements, patriotic songs; and everywhere the watchful eyes of the "late great leader and Chairman Mao Tse-tung," and his successor Chairman Hua Kuo-feng, "the wise leader."

The hospital-waiting-room quality of the border station was increased by stacks of pamphlets and magazines, but this hospital did not even have an out-of-date *Newsweek* or *National Geographic*. It gave a foretaste of the monotony in reading materials I was to find in the New China. Everything had been published in Peking: Mao essays; poems by "peasants, soldiers, and workers"; glossy pictorial supplements filled with stories of the People's Heroes, from the Five-Good Soldier to the Five-Shovel Brigade of housewives; and horror stories of slave keeping in Tibet.

In California, where gurus and lamas flourish, it would be impossible to imagine that Tibetan monks kept slaves—according to the magazine, it happened until a few years ago.

The magazines were filled with statistics, an avalanche of information that later would become such a tiresome aspect of my Chinese experience. Even the simplest question I might ask seemed always to provoke a response that included incredible tales of land reclamation, steel production, agricultural yields—everything in billions of yuan and millions of *jins* of grain or *mu* of land.

Was the hour-long wait for the train a useful decompression period for the visitors, a time to set aside some American prejudices? Or was it a deliberate attempt to program us with the first of those infuriating pep talks, to convince us that we were entering paradise, a land where thieves are reformed, murderers do not exist, and where the only gunfire heard is the sound of blanks used in militia target practice. . . . I was no closer to the answers when I left China three months later.

But the train arrived, and I saw the first of many contradictions that lay ahead. Its "hard" and "soft" seats were a reminder that class differences are not wiped out simply by a change of name. Even in the People's Republic, foreigners and Chinese officials have swivel chairs, pots of flowers, little shaded table lamps, solicitous attendants offering tea.

The train journey itself was an anticlimax—its scenes had already been described by too many other travelers. Fields rolled past the window, looking much like those on the Hong Kong side of the border. Some of the figures in the landscape might have stepped out of an old Hollywood movie: water buffalo; workers hand-hoeing in a field; a man pulling a cart along a country road, using a shoulder harness that could have been in use a hundred years ago. And the distant houses look more like the walled villages near Kowloon than the soaring concrete blocks in the Shanghai suburbs that Eileen had described.

But if the magazines at the border are to be believed, nothing is what it seems. Children in the schoolyard (seeming no different from those in California) are said to assemble electronic components or to run a railroad. That figure with hand hoe will join his friends after work to write and produce a miniopera.

A kind of paranoia sets in. Is the business-suited passenger reading the London *Economist* across the aisle perhaps a former Tibetan slave? Did the smartly dressed girl shepherding the foreign tourists herd real sheep or camels once upon a time? Is the old fellow nodding over a book a soldier-hero in disguise? Or perhaps the oilfields' original Iron Man?

No wonder the journey passed so quickly. And then it was time to bring my thoughts back to reality, as the moving picture outside the windows stopped too. The scene came into focus. The train pulled in. . . .

2

FAMILY TIES

CANTON is like Queens, I thought, arriving for a visit with unknown aunts and uncles. It reminded me of the time when I flew across the United States to stay with relatives. Glad to have a place to stay, to have more knowledgeable guides than most tourists do, but also thinking about Mother's reminders: "Don't give Auntie any trouble. . . ." You can never quite escape the feeling of being cooped up with relations, wishing there were a bit more time for freewheeling on your own.

The platform at Canton was just as confusing as the arrival gates at Kennedy Airport had been, and even more crowded. The faces that had seemed so familiar in a dozen photographs were nowhere to be seen. I was on my own after all. And then, out of the crowd, a woman who appeared to be a complete stranger rushed forward, flinging her arms around me; heads turned as other family voices joined in; and, just as in New York, the fuss made me feel like a circus sideshow.

34

Quickly the resemblance to New York faded, and the picture seemed to assume the quality of a dream. The man on a bicycle, those children sweeping a sidewalk, the colonial buildings lining the tree-shaded riverfront—I had never seen them before, but each scene faithfully recalled the photos or slides I had seen of travelers who had walked the street before of me.

How could the pictures be so faithfully duplicated, the same figures appear in appointed roles, without some careful behind-the-scenes manipulating? Perhaps it was only a

Buildings that once housed colonial administrators and Western businessmen along the Pearl River in Canton. Note the light traffic, even at five in the afternoon in the heart of the city.

movie set—the buildings false, the figures directed by off-stage PRC officials?

Trying to make conversation with relatives known only from letters added to my sense of unreality. As I asked foolish questions, stock answers inevitably followed.

"What happened to the families whose sampans used to line the river?"

Straight from the border-station pamphlets came the answer—a jumble of phrases that told me how happy the "poor" boat people were relocated in a concrete workers' flat.

"And the beggars my mother remembered?" I learned that they have a new life working for the future of the People's Republic of China.

Probably everyone else was nervous too, even the cousin carrying my suitcase and the uncle who insisted on using his Hong Kong business English to give me the stock how-was-your-journey quiz.

But this was not, after all, the stock welcome one receives in an American city. The family had no car waiting, we made no detours for hamburgers to provide us with strength for a long journey home. Here, as at the border, I was on my own two feet, in a steaming Canton afternoon of late spring. In comparison with New York streets, Renmin (People's) Road and Jiefang (Liberation) Road seemed bucolic, yet in spite of the fact that bicycles outnumbered cars, the streets were not as pollution-free as the Chinese had claimed.

Nor were the people the look-alike figures I had expected to see marching through the streets. If my first impression was a horrified I-have-seen-this-before, I soon realized that the scene in its own way was as richly varied as Hong Kong.

Canton retains its reputation for being fashion conscious. In this cosmopolitan city, the baggy jackets and trousers of commune wear would be out of place. The weather is much too hot for the dark gray Mao (or Sun Yat-sen) jackets of Peking's streets. Open-necked white shirts and dark slacks make more sense. Girls returning from their weekday workshift wore bright blue and yellow and red cotton dresses, which gave them a festive air.

We turned another corner, and suddenly there was a lovely red gate, leading into a small courtyard. I saw tiled roofs. . . . The stereotypes of PRC propaganda disappeared. I have come home!

In some ways, that was the most unreal moment of all, in spite of the photos sent by Uncle Chen. Perhaps those magazines at the border had programmed me to expect another Standard Chinese household: Momma Chen, Poppa Chen, the inevitable two Little Chens—all living in a two-room flat, with the parents going off two by two to work each morning.

Instead, I found myself in the tree-shaded courtyard, straight from a Hollywood movie of Old China. Doors opened off the central court, tempting spicy steam floated out of a window, someone was practicing on the flute. A bird sang.

When I finally had everyone sorted out later, I knew there were actually seven families living in the various apartments opening onto the inner court—all related in some way, with each family allotted between two and five rooms. In the old days, one family lived here with its servants, and the man's concubines and their children occupied the other apartments.

I wished then that a lifetime of inhibitions about asking forthright questions did not prevent me from asking what I so badly wanted to know: How had the Chens managed to retain this fine piece of real estate—occupying, if

Many families in Canton still live in traditional tiled-roof houses around small courtyards or crowded along narrow lanes, with much of the everyday life, including cooking, carried on outdoors.

not owning, it any longer—in the newly egalitarian republic? Perhaps Uncle's seat on the local party committee had something to do with it. . . . But that was a point on which even my father, after I got back to California, could not enlighten me.

They made room for me in the main apartment—the only one with an unoccupied bed, recently vacated by a cousin who had graduated from middle school and then been sent down to the commune that his grandfather had been so glad to leave.

It is luxurious living by local standards, although it bears little resemblance to an American home. There are no beanbag chairs or conversation corners, no big speakers or TV console—none of the things we take for granted. All bedrooms are shared. Instead of California's two and a half baths for the household, there is only one bathroom, plus a separate toilet, for all seven families. There is only one proper kitchen to be shared by all, although each family has a corner for a small cookstove and a place for the kettle and a thermos jug of water for making tea.

It is a relief to see that the Canton family still has rose-wood chairs and tables, carved beds, porcelain bowls, cloisonné vases, hanging scrolls. The small Tientsin carpet that was part of Auntie Chen's dowry, silk cushions, a jade tree in a glass case—all are like the Chinese antiques we have at home in California.

Even the carved table looks as though it had been set for one of the family banquets at home. It reminds me of special occasions at home, when older members fuss about serving the "correct" dishes for wedding, funeral, or New Year ceremonies. Of course, many of the younger cousins in California are careless about observing the rules, rather like some Jewish friends I have who shock their parents when they stop keeping a kosher household.

That first evening, the food was all spread out on the carved table: porcelain soup spoons and bowls; platters of "square tiger-tails" (squid); three kinds of "meat" (in Western usage, poultry—chicken, duck, squab).

All my favorite dishes . . . And as the aunts urged me to taste the goodies, cousins reached for tidbits with their chopsticks, and the uncles talked back and forth as though the rest of us had not been there, I could concentrate on the food and take a closer look at the family I had come so far to see.

Eating is serious business in China—even the restaurants put all their talents into the food and scorn the Western habit of fancy decor. So I could enjoy the privilege of getting the "bird-brain"—the choicest morsel of the duck's head (always served whole), which crowned the dish of chopped duck meat with ginger, mushrooms, tiger-lily buds, and "tree ears."

Smiling and nodding as great-grandmamas always seem to do, the eldest Chen—or was it one of the Wang branch, or the Fongs?—spooned up her shark-fin soup, making the most of this special-occasion treat. A swarm of small cousins from the other six households giggled and watched me—I think they hoped to see if the odd foreign relation really did know how to eat bird's-nest soup or to respond graciously when Auntie Fong reached toward the whole fish and picked up the "best" part to offer her guest: glittering fisheyes. Plum sauce, rice, pork, five-flavor salt . . . no wonder so many foreigners returning from China talk about the food more than about their visits to communes and to hydroelectric projects.

It was nice to realize that bare-bones Communist style hasn't yet spread to the table. Even the "eight-jewel" dishes are still served, although eight-treasure porridge is more often called simply eight-taste now (pork loin, pork kidney, bamboo shoots, fish-skin, pork tendon, mushrooms, sea cucumber, scallops).

By the time we got to the last course—not a Western dessert, but always something sweet and sour, and on this occasion a large sweet-and-sour fish—some of the personalities were beginning to emerge.

There was the cranky uncle, picking at the special treats and making unfavorable comparisons with the way Grandma prepared the dishes back in rural Kwangtung. There always seems to be a shy cousin, whose eyes remain fixed on the food. But if only there were not always an auntie to tell everyone how "cute" a niece or nephew looked at the age of five, sitting down fully clothed in a seaside puddle. Still, that is better than the uncle at a San Francisco wedding banquet who insisted on telling everyone his "puddle" story—how he had picked up the bride (then six months old), and the dreadful effect on his new suit. . . .

Gradually the eating slowed, and we slipped into family chitchat—greetings from the network of relatives in California and New York, news of jobs and weddings and newly arrived cousins. Finally, it was time to clear the table —with the aunts refusing to let the guest help.

But the guest was also the family's very own American-bearing-gifts. Like most Canton families with American connections, everyone at this table had become a remittance man (or woman). Foreign travelers' tales and press releases from Peking seem to ignore this particular fact of modern Chinese life, the relations who send dollars back to China, just as the first emigrants did a century or more ago.

Reports from China show a watch costing 80 yuan on the wrist of a worker who earns less than 100 yuan (about sixty dollars) a month (after twenty-four years as a factory worker), yet who also has a camera that cost two months' wages and a radio that represents several weeks' work. Captions refer to the "new wealth" of the workers. I wonder how much of this wealth really comes from overseas remittances.

My family in California is far from rich—especially when the plant temporarily lays off workers. Yet to the family in Canton, our $1,500 a month makes us seem like millionaires. Perhaps that is why they still seem to take so literally the old name for San Francisco: Kam Shan, the Mountain of Gold.

Playing Santa Claus in the month of May was a new experience for me. It would be unfair to feel cynical about the ever-extended hands of relatives—even when they later seemed to assume that I was their personal banker whenever we went out to eat, or they accompanied me on souvenir-buying trips.

Everyone was delighted with the presents, as pleased as though the packages contained a rare piece of jade instead of two modern treasures, a small camera and a very modest radio–tape recorder.

There are still relatively few individual tape recorders or record players in the PRC. Even the radios are apt to be low-fidelity plastic horrors. Privately owned TV sets are even more scarce—virtually nonexistent, even among the workers in the Shanghai factory that makes them. Considering that one small black-and-white set costs more than three months' wages, the sixteen-inch model more than twice that much, it is easy to see why television sets are usually community-owned, the property of a factory, production team, or school.

What would the evenings be like without the familiar TV entertainment? After growing up in a world where children learn to recite television jingles before they read primers, it was hard to imagine how we would pass the time— although it did not take me long to discover that for most of the Canton relations, there was no such concept as "spare" time.

That first evening, exhausted by the effort of so much conversation in Cantonese (and the classroom English my younger cousins insisted on trying out), I was relieved when a solicitious auntie thought I might want to go to bed early.

It is always difficult to sleep in a strange bed. In China, the problem is compounded by the fact that no one has the luxury of a private room. Even the dictionary defines privacy as "living in retirement or seclusion." Two children to a room—and even two to a bed—is commonplace. Many apartments provide only a curtain to separate sections for children and parents or other older family members. I counted myself lucky to have only one roommate, even though in California I would be less than happy to share quarters with a pesky twelve-year-old.

Sleep—and the pretense of sleep—provided my only really private moments in the following weeks. Lying awake that first night, trying to sort out the impressions, I also tried to prepare myself for the difficulties to come.

There was my mother's advice to remember: "Do not be uncouth. Don't talk politics. Wait and see how they do things. Let your uncles volunteer answers, but never ask questions yourself." I had already experienced the silent treatment when I questioned the uncle who had worked in Hong Kong about how he would "like" the forthcoming transfer back to an assignment out in rural Kwangtung. He could chat in English, but he simply smiled and remained silent.

Westerners often blame this kind of response on some peculiarly "inscrutable" Chinese trait—or they speak of a "Chinese wall of silence." Many of my friends find it strange that I do not care to talk about my sex life or even to discuss with strangers the latest behavior of a group of teenage Chinese delinquents. Yet during my summer in England, I discovered that the Chinese are not the only ones who give a "freezing" response to any question they do not wish to answer. The English are experts at the silent treatment too.

Would the typical reaction to questions make it impossible for me to go beyond the slender information of college courses back in the United States or Chinese press releases, and find out for myself what the Chinese scene was really like?

For there was always the daunting realization that no

one can see more than a very, very small pinhead in the vast Chinese landscape. It is easy to feel superior when ignorant tourists mistake a single figure in a five-*mu* field for a "representative of the entire Republic." But could I really make a more accurate sampling?

After all, China stretches 5,000 kilometers from east to west, 5,500 kilometers from north to south. The weeks in Kwangtung Province, even if I crisscrossed it a dozen times, would tell me nothing of the dry highlands of Tibet towering 4,000 to 6,000 meters above sea level. Kwangtung is in the fertile rice-growing south, where 2,000 millimeters of rain falls in an average year. But what of the life-style in the Taklamakan Desert, where 10 millimeters would be a wet year?

And the variety of people. Even talking to Eileen, I had wondered how much the 11 million residents of Shanghai and the 2 million of Canton have in common. Or how closely their thoughts agree with the ideas of the 38 million "fraternal nationalities" and ethnic groups who are not even what most foreigners think of as "Chinese."

China's twenty-two provinces and five autonomous regions include a dizzying variety of races. They include 1.5 million Mongols—formerly herders of sheep and camels, but now just as likely to be computer technologists or experts in scientific livestock management. There are the Miao, traditionally wearing black turbans, silver bangles, many necklaces, but today there are white-smocked Miao working in nuclear research and advanced petroleum engineering. Other groups resemble Russian Cossacks, in tunics and high leather boots. The Sinkiang Uighur Autonomous Region (organized in 1955) bordering Pakistan, the Soviet Union, and Afghanistan has Turkic Uighurs and eleven other minorities—including Uzbeks, Kazakhs, and Tatars. Yunnan Province has twenty-one "minorities" (a term denoting special privileges rather than discrimination in China today). None of these groups would understand a single word of the Canton family's dialect.

Even if it were possible to travel throughout the vast distances of China, could anyone master all the languages needed to talk to these peoples? Or talk to even a tiny sampling of the 98 percent of the Chinese people classified as true Han?

"Han" is a name derived from a dynasty that ruled from about 200 B.C. to about A.D. 220—about the same time that Roman culture was at its height. China still includes much of the same territory as it did then—although Vietnam is now independent, and other regions have been annexed within China's borders. My family has often described regional stereotypes—the "dour" people of Peking, with snobbish attitudes toward "coarse" southerners, for instance. Eileen says there are still playboys lingering in the streets of Shanghai, long after the wild life of the old International Settlement vanished. Elderly businessmen, fresh-off-the-boat newcomers, young gangsters, and third-generation political activists within the small area of San Francisco's Chinatown all think differently from one another, too. . . .

Surely the Chinese are not quite so uniform in outlook as the news features from Peking claim, even if the citizens of the PRC are no longer divided politically (as so many Chinese families in the United States were) by the choice between support of Chiang Kai-shek and of Mao.

Lying in bed that first night, wondering about my discoveries of the coming days, I began to think about the ways in which the modern scene differed from my parents' memories of the Old China, and to wonder if the Chinese history I had studied in school would really be helpful.

Like Eileen, I know that China did not leap overnight

from the primitive pastoral scenes glimpsed from the train window to the advances represented by nuclear power, vast oil reserves, and sophisticated communications satellites. But Eileen had found that the foreign visitor who believes that all "advances" are due to the thoughts of Chairman Mao may be better received in modern China than the visitor who takes pride in the ancient Chinese heritage.

I cannot discount China's past cultural and technological leadership. Past achievements have sustained members of my family in the face of Western discrimination. Sneered at as "coolies" in California less than fifty years ago, they could remember how Marco Polo admired the advanced living standards of their ancestors: clean streets; hot and cold baths; food eaten daintily with chopsticks at a time when Europeans were still dipping bare hands into a common stewpot. . . .

I am proud of China's contributions—not only the "simple" contribution of Asia's staple diet of tea and rice, but also the sophistication of an advanced culture. My ancestors provided a written language for the peoples of Japan, Korea, and Vietnam (rural workers in China have dug up fragments of writing on silk and bamboo dated about 2000 B.C.). The Chinese were first in many fields of art, literature, music. China was the route by which Buddhism spread from India through most of Asia; it was the source of Taoism; the home of the philosopher Confucius, whose teachings underlie the manners and governments of many countries.

What a pity that the modern People's Republic has tried to discredit Confucian ethics and the achievements of the past. They talk only about the inventions of workers today—supposedly "inspired by our great leader," Chairman Mao. They do not say much about the long-ago Chinese who already had instruments of astronomy, who made fine porcelain while Europeans were still eating off wooden platters, who invented such aids to comfortable living as eyeglasses and umbrellas.

As I lay awake that first evening, longing for a big glass of milk or a late-night snack (cures for insomnia back home), I wished that one other ancient Chinese invention were still popular in its land of origin: doggie bags. As Martin de Rada noted in 1575, whenever there was food left over after a banquet: "We were given it to carry away in hampers."

But the banquet that welcomed me to Canton had not featured a bedtime doggie bag. Already I had made a discovery so often overlooked by the tourists who are shepherded through China in cocooned hotel luxury: the impressive statistics and the showpiece living quarters are quickly reduced to their proper scale when you become part of the picture yourself.

Reports of three hundred aqueducts bringing hydroelectric power to remote corners of the republic are less impressive when you are trapped in a household with no refrigerator to raid.

3

THE STREETS
OF CANTON

I WENT OUT on the streets of
Canton next morning—streets that seem less "Chinese"
than Hong Kong's or even San Francisco's Chinatown, the
clean and crime-free streets so highly praised by Western
travelers. My dad would have been delighted.

He is always saying, when bubble gum glues his feet
to downtown brick sidewalks, as he stands amid a litter of
beer cans and hamburger wrappers: "Why do we have to
pay a man fifteen thousand dollars a year to keep the streets
so dirty?"

In Canton, they claim that they pay nothing at all.
Millions of volunteer sweepers keep Chinese streets clean.
But they do pay a price, a price too high for me—the lock-
step life that begins at dawn each day.

On the first morning in Canton, I found myself in a
household where everyone had a purpose. In the Chen family, everyone followed an appointed pattern: jobs, schools,
neighborhood committees. Even the eldest great-aunt did

The street clean-up brigade. Girl in foreground wears checked shirt, and workers in background wear cotton work suits.

her bit, putting in several hours at a "service center" for neighborhood mending and laundry.

It was impossible to be a lie-abed—and later it seemed that the entire neighborhood had conspired to make sure that I got swept along with the crowd. But for that first week, I could escape the constraints and venture outdoors to take a look at the Canton streets on my own—although the distressed aunts fussed, fearing all sorts of possible trouble in which I could find myself.

Trying to blend in with the crowds was difficult. Thousands of workers walked along or rode bicycles or buses, all with a purpose, eyes fixed on the job or meeting ahead. I hoped that no one would recognize me as an idle American.

First discovery: The streets were not quite so clean as the legend would have us believe. Early in the morning, before the armies of volunteer broom pushers were out and about, I could see litter here and there. Later, I often saw the parks and areas around apartment houses littered with a holiday carpet of candy wrappers or red firecracker paper.

But China is not our throwaway world. There are no beer cans and soft-drink cans to discard. Bottles are reused. This is a country without the litter that accompanies junk food, takeout milk shakes and hamburgers, coffee-dispensing machines, potato-chip bags, taco counters. Food scraps are carefully collected to feed the pigs.

What about the tales of crime-free streets? Other parts of the world may be safe. Eileen had experienced the crime-free streets of Tokyo. I had hitchhiked through Europe without danger. Even in Hong Kong, where local papers printed several stories about Triad membership (a cross between old-style tongs and modern Mafia), Eileen and I had felt safe as long as we stayed away from areas where young toughs hang out.

At home in San Francisco, there were a hundred murders in the first nine months of 1977. This score included Chinese squabbles over turf (much like similar fights in Chicago or New York), as well as battles over the (illegal) fireworks concession, and a spectacular massacre that left five people (Chinese, Japanese, Caucasian) dead.

My father is a cynic. He says that he knows why Canton's streets are so free of crime: "They have shipped all their misfits to California, to beef up our Chinatown gangs."

It is true that some Chinese misfits have sneaked across the border into Hong Kong and then found their way to Western cities. But if they are caught committing crimes

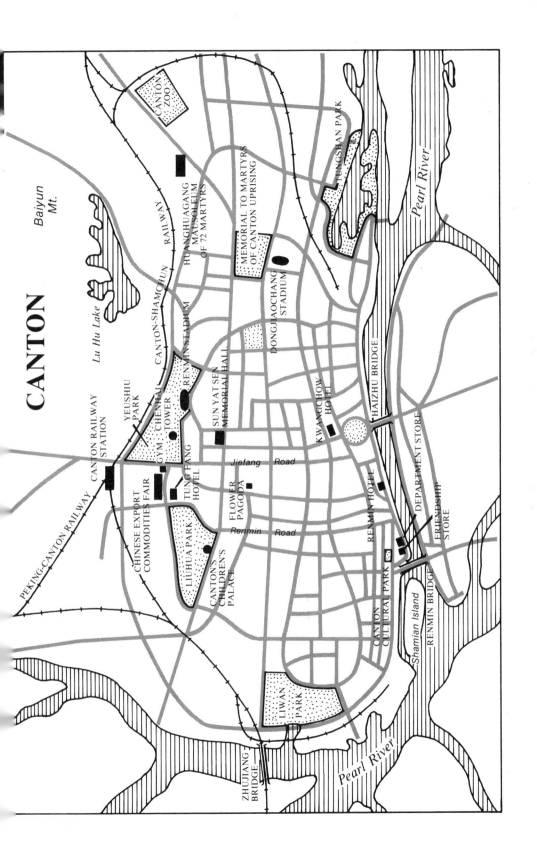

in Canton, they are "re-educated" Chinese-style—sent out to labor at distant work sites, breaking rocks not in the Western-style prison yard but "making fields out of mountains" or "constructing a channel to bring water to the desert."

I enjoyed the unfamiliar pleasure of wandering the streets without having to watch out for muggers and pickpockets. But I did not like the feeling that I was back in high school, with bells ringing and teachers ordering students to hurry to class. Here in Canton, the reminders came from loudspeakers and huge posters. The lecturing voices also roared at me from the insufferable heroes of patriotic films and operas.

In place of the school watchdogs or anxious parents asking, "Who brought you home at eleven last night?" the Chinese have neighborhood committees and other beady-eyed busybodies waiting to "admonish" anyone guilty of dropping a scrap of orange peel or a nonconformist who tries to carry out an experiment in petty crime.

Members of these committees (also known as "street" or "lane" committees) are often retired workers looking for something useful to do. In the PRC everyone regards our Western ideas of "leisure activities" and even the recreation at senior-citizen centers as both eccentric and selfish.

No matter how old you are, there is work to be done. Grannies and grandfathers alike can do their bit in the service centers, nurseries, and volunteer clean-up crews. They act as twenty-four-hour watchdogs. They admonish traffic offenders, warn children not to play in the streets, and apply group pressures to any kind of public nuisance. They even run annual campaigns, such as "Fight Disease" and "Eliminate Flies."

Some of the more naïve travelers have come back from China claiming that the streets are so safe that anyone can leave market stalls unattended or bicycles unlocked. I did not see a single bicycle left anywhere except in the public bike racks, watched by a guardian-checker and firmly chained down with its own individual padlock. No one in his right mind leaves a bicycle out overnight. Such a precious possession is exposed neither to a would-be thief nor to the rain that might fall in the night.

Common sense rather than the "thoughts of Chairman Mao Tse-tung" seems to be more effective in keeping the crime rate low. Communists are not saints. The hectoring neighborhood committees cannot always catch a thief. Nor are the streets quite as idyllic as the main boulevards often appear. There are still some slummy areas and even quite a few rootless young idlers.

Eileen had warned me that the streets of Canton and Shanghai have more than their share of floaters. She says that they are usually city kids who cannot stand the life out in the country—where the PRC tells them it is their duty to work. So they sneak back to the brighter (not much brighter!) lights of the city and spend their days squatting on the sidewalks playing cards (until they are chased off by neighborhood committee aunties). They pick up money where they can, such as by picking up someone else's radio or bike if they get the opportunity.

Anyone who drops out of the job that he is supposed to be doing has only two choices: hang about on the streets, or go over the border into Hong Kong. . . .

I had my doubts about the happy streets of Canton before the first morning was over. A tough-looking boy, a grubby sixteen-year-old by his appearance, slouched out of an alley and stopped in front of me. His accent was so filled with strange rural tones that I could scarcely understand a word at first. Was it a holdup? I couldn't see a knife or gun. After all, there was no danger. He was just like a skid-row panhandler back home at the bus depot, asking for some small change. The boy must have spotted my out-of-towner style, or perhaps he had learned the advantage of stopping anyone in American-made jeans.

Perhaps if I had paid for his lunch, he would have filled me in on the seamy side of Canton life. But the caution of my aunts and that inhibiting sense of family responsibility made me say, "No money!"

Conforming to the tea-drinking habit was easy enough. Tea is our favorite drink at home, and the instant coffee my aunts so solicitously provided was horrible enough to convert the staunchest coffee drinker to tea.

Why is it that so few visitors to China comment on the deadening effects of conformity in even the smallest detail of daily life? Perhaps it is because most tourists are cocooned, glassed in at lavish hotels, where they have no knowledge of the separate (and unequal) breakfasts of their interpreters.

Before my eyes were fully opened on the first day, I had already sampled the flat taste of the simple life. In the morning cousins grabbed a stuffed bun or a piece of pastry that is a cross between a doughnut and a slice of fried bread. Some of the adults went off to eat the very cheap breakfast at the factory cafeteria. I was left with Granny, to share the staple breakfast of thin, dull, gray rice "porridge."

Even a confirmed breakfast skipper like me soon longs for the choices offered by American refrigerators and cupboards: juice, cereals, waffles, fried or scrambled eggs, bacon, buttered toast, pastries filled with apples or fragrant with sprinkled cinnamon, sausages, ham. . . . Those spartan breakfasts of buns or porridge were in discouraging contrast to the lavish feast of my welcome to Canton.

Outside the windows each morning I could see the

early-morning exercises that always impress Western visitors. Long before jogging became popular in the United States, everyone in China from nursery-school babies to octogenarians seemed to be out exercising on the predawn streets. Groups of workers competed in marathon races around the perimeter of Peking. Every schoolyard, office, and factory had its quota doing morning calisthenics. Young workers and old grannies alike were practicing *t'ai chi ch'uan,* while schoolchildren often worked off surplus energy with the more vigorous *shao lin.*

Wu shu practice. Although the words *wu shu* identify the traditional "martial arts," these graceful exercises look more like Western dance routines.

The Westerners might have seen some similar activity at home if they had known where to look: in San Francisco's Portsmouth Square, I saw groups practice *t'ai chi* at five thirty in the morning, sometimes accompanied by their eighty-year-old teacher.

My *t'ai chi* teacher says: "Miss one day of practice, and you lose ten." So I never miss an opportunity to run through the basic moves—even though this "shadow boxing" often draws odd looks from other people standing in line for the movies or waiting for a concert to begin. But I can practice whenever and wherever I choose; at home I do not have to work out along with the group.

The few days before I was caught up in the group life of Canton—before the family had quite figured out how to keep me correctly employed—gave me a chance to do some unsupervised people watching.

The Cantonese do not pay much attention to odd-looking strangers. They have seen foreign traders for centuries —even before Marco Polo traveled along the Silk Road to the city of the Khans (Peking) in the thirteenth century. When the Ming edict closed China's borders in 1430, Canton was the only place where foreigners and Chinese merchants could trade, until the doors reopened officially in 1720. During those years, the Chinese continued to regard all foreigners as barbarians. Nevertheless the Canton Merchants Guild used to trade with them most courteously and even without written contracts.

So, too, in the twentieth century. Merchants came to the Export Commodities Trade Fair every spring and summer, even before diplomatic channels were reopened. Today, foreign visitors are so commonplace in Canton that it is the only city where one recent traveler reasserted the old saw: "Familiarity definitely breeds contempt."

There are many cosmopolitan visitors, with Hong

Kong so close—no wonder that the city has always had a reputation for high fashion. Yet the sharpest dressers I saw in Canton followed neither American nor French fashions. Men with bare chests draped with golden chains, girls in long dresses, beads, and bare midriffs, anyone wearing platform soles would not meet with local approval. And I am sure that if I had gone down the street smelling of after-shave or cologne, I would soon have been given a lecture by a neighborhood-committee auntie.

My American T-shirt was exotic by local standards, but even if I did not quite sing in tune, I did at least look Chinese. After a couple of hours of self-conscious wandering (the only one in the crowds who seemed not to be moving purposefully about some errand), I thought it would be nice to continue the people watching from the safety of a local noodle shop.

That was not as easy as you might suppose. Like my relations, most adults eat lunch on the job. The typical Chinese restaurant is often better suited to family or business parties, to large groups rather than the lone diner. And the range of fast-food outlets that we take for granted in the United States is unknown in China.

The closest one can find to convenience foods is "plate food." These ready-assembled combination plates are useful for families who work late, consisting of uncooked meat and vegetables (prechopped or sliced), sometimes with a portion of noodles. All that is left to do is a few minutes' home cooking. I couldn't even find a place selling *dim sum,* the marvelous bite-size snacks so popular for light meals in Hong Kong and San Francisco, although a famous garden restaurant in Canton has a chef known for his 1,000 varieties.

Two or three times I tried to ask someone in the hurrying crowd for directions to a place for lunch. But as soon as

Two small shops that supply snacks for Canton's workers. People can buy bottled drinks and candy at the left-hand shop (individually wrapped candies, weighed out, and sold in a twist of paper for a few fen). At the shop to the right, which sells ice-cream bars, are several soldiers (background).

I opened my mouth they identified me as an outsider, and that always seemed to provoke an almost paranoid response. It was always: "I don't know"—even to the simplest request for directions. (That is, if I could even persuade the person to "see" the annoying foreigner in the first place.) But then, have you ever tried to ask the way in New York?

Finally I spotted one of the noodle shops Uncle had described, where they price noodles the way some restau-

rants price steak at home, by weight. Later in the week I
was able to track down the other local lunch offerings, even
one that could almost pass for a burrito (a thin pancake or
a lettuce leaf rolled around fillings of ground squab and
vegetables in the Chinese version), and of course the infinite variety of everyday soups.

Eating is supposed to be done like everything else—
efficiently, with no wasted time or motion. I could not sit
and linger over a cup of tea. But thanks to the custom of
communal tables, I became a practiced eavesdropper during the next few days.

But eavesdropping was a rather disappointing occupation. Perhaps the middle-aged men at the next table were
cautious when they heard my not-quite-local accent. Two
teenagers (surely they ought to have been at school?) may
have had their own reasons for spending their noodle time
discussing chances of victory in a forthcoming athletic
meet. . . .

Some fragments seemed more outspoken than comments later made to me directly, including scraps of
grumbling talk by two separate groups suffering under
cranky work-team leaders. Another group sounded as
though they were planning some public criticism with Big
Character posters, a favorite device for attacking anyone
who does not keep to the party line (more on this in Chapter 5). One girl, apparently a late starter to join her group
down on the commune, was unhappy about leaving her
friends. Judging by the teasing comments of her companion, there might even have been a spot of (frustrated) romance involved—the friend she would miss most appeared
to be a boy.

Perhaps I missed some of the nuances of these overheard conversations. But there was no mistaking the horrified looks of people at neighboring tables when I tried to

strike up a conversation with a girl who sat dipping up her soup alone. She kept her eyes on the bowl—and fled from the table as soon as it was empty, while an elderly couple also seated at our table made pointed comments about the oafish behavior of "modern young people."

Later, when I had spent two weeks on the commune, I had a better understanding of just how uncouth my friendly attempts had seemed. For I discovered in the country that China's liberated worker-women still seem to prefer to huddle together in segregated groups, whether they are on their way to work in the fields or just looking for a place to sit while they watch the outdoor evening movie.

No matter where I lunched, though, I never heard anything resembling the political arguments of a campus coffeehouse back home. And I missed the give-and-take of groups of people my own age, eating together and talking freely while doing so. Only when I met some of my cousins' workmates did I begin to understand the seeming coldness of the streets and shops of Canton, in which I always felt myself an outsider. Everyone prefers group activity, and I belonged to no group.

But I did enjoy walking alone, especially when I realized that the pedestrian is king. Traffic is not quite as light as it seems to be in photos of Peking's endless streams of bicycles. Buses and trucks contribute to noise pollution. But there are no school buses. Everyone walks. Instead of panel trucks, there are lots of pedal-power carts—a flatbed hitched behind a bicycle. I was surprised to see one carrying crates of milk bottles (not a popular beverage in China). However, it turned out to be a hotel delivery and partly meant for ice cream.

There are no private automobiles. The Chinese were conscious of the gasoline engine's wastefulness long before we in the West began to worry about dwindling oil re-

A surge of bicycles marks the end of the afternoon shift, when workers crowd onto buses and even the backs of trucks.

serves. Even now that they have newly discovered oil at Taching, the Chinese prefer to use available supplies for industry, for mechanizing agriculture, and to increase food production.

I did get to know one driver—the younger Wang cousin. It seemed odd to realize that he had not shared my experiences of car ownership and driver education while he was still in school. Like most drivers in China, he had only taken lessons after he needed to handle an auto on the job. However, he had to pass the world's toughest test before he started his Travel Service work—not only were his eyes, hearing, and blood pressure tested, but he also had to undergo a thorough exam on mechanical ability, and had to show that he could dismantle and reassemble the entire engine, if necessary.

Traffic laws favor the pedestrian, and a driver's license can be revoked in circumstances that might not even rate a ticket in the United States. Again, the neighborhood committee is active—deciding compensation for the (rare) accident victim, with a "sentence" that sometimes forces the culprit to move in with the victim (especially if it is an older person without nonworking relatives) and perform nursing chores until the invalid recovers. In the West, such a sentence would probably put the victim in double jeop-

A group of girls on their way to the Children's Palace for sports and other activities. Each wears the scarf of the Little Red Guards (renamed Young Pioneers in 1978).

ardy; we are continually warned to double-bar our doors and never to admit strangers. My Western eye looks doubtfully on these virtuous involuntary nursemaids. Do they never escalate their crime to include ripoff or rape?

As I moved through the streets of Canton and priced some of the items in the shops, I was continually amazed that the local citizens did *not* resort to crime. No wonder that so many relatives who recite lessons about "bureaucrat capitalists" are happy to accept presents purchased with "capitalist" profits from the Golden Mountain of San Francisco.

When Cousin Li starts work next year, he will have to pay two weeks' wages for a simple suit. An alarm clock to wake him up for work would cost five days' labor. At 25 yuan, the personal transistor radio that American teenagers take for granted remains completely beyond his reach.

Nor are goods as readily available as you might suppose from all those pictures of happy workers wearing watches, carrying cameras, tuning in radios. Not only did I find myself paying for many extras that the family could not afford out of a two-adult salary (ranging between 120 and 200 yuan, depending on the work assignment of that particular couple), I also found myself fronting in the purchase of preferred brands of cigarettes. For a while it even looked as though I would have to go out and buy a sewing machine.

Luckily, the name of the recently married Wang cousins came to the top of a list for a sewing machine before I was driven to buy one. But I was really surprised to discover how often family and friends had to sign up and wait their turn for things—especially a bicycle or watch—that I had thought readily available to anyone who could manage to save up the cash. As a tourist, I could go in and buy things right off the floor. My family, even when they did have the money, could not always buy what they wanted, although more goods will be available in 1979, and they could not buy some of the luxury items and antiques that are available to foreigners.

In the circumstances, keeping stores open seven days a week and until late at night did not seem necessary. Yet the department store where the family bought clothing, household items, and cloth was always crowded. Gradually, I also learned to look for the little shops that resembled the old-style markets of Hong Kong and San Francisco.

There I found shoppers buying candied plums and cherries from Peking, noodles, rice, meat substitutes such as "soy chicken," dried fishlips, lengths of pig intestine, a fish swimming in its own take-home baggie. In odd corners, a few of the old craftsmen survived: assembling a cal- ligraphy brush, carving a seal, making red-and-white paper cutouts—although such traditional paper designs as drag- ons and jade princesses seemed to have been replaced by sets of "popular sports" and children shown busily sweep- ing up "old cultural objects."

My pleasant freedom to wander the streets ended when my cousin came back from his latest assignment shepherding foreigners on a two-week tour. His motives were kindly, but I learned to dread the times when he was home, because he always insisted that I would learn more if I followed the paths laid down for ordinary overseas visi- tors. I went along with several of these groups to visit workers' apartments. But I was bored by the monotony of conversations that sounded like memorized speeches—al- though my cousin insisted they were spontaneous.

I could have given a pretty fair description of the in- side of one of these apartments even before my first in- spection tour (and even without going to China at all, if I looked at the thousands of words and pictures flooding

out of Peking). There is a certain curiosity value in seeing
how someone else lives. But whether your own home is in
the ghetto or in a suburban ranch house with swimming
pool, the first reaction of an American visitor to the average
Chinese apartment is that it is unbelievably small and bare.

The Chu family home on our itinerary was exactly
what I had expected: the regulation two rooms, each about
ten by fourteen feet; several families sharing each available
bathroom and kitchen; the rooms lighted with a single un-
shaded lightbulb, too dim for reading, or a harsh fluorescent
bar; a big double bed in one corner serving as couch by
day; a second room with additional beds and chairs lined up
with geometric precision against a wall; a large table doing
triple duty for meals, homework, and sewing; few decorations; the general appearance almost institutional. Yet the
colored enamel washbowls, yellow blankets, flowered quilts,
a red alarm clock, embroidered mats—and the friendly
welcome with cups of tea—left a pleasant impression.

Some of my aunts chided me when I sounded critical
of the frugal life-style. They reminded me of the hardships
of earlier generations and pointed out the practical value
of bare floors, which stay cool during Canton's muggy sum-
mers. The stark "model" homes, though, are kept that way
not out of practical considerations but for ideological reasons. Party officials may have curtains at the windows of
their limousines, but homes and hotels are supposed to be
strictly no-frills. Criticism of Chairman Mao's widow
Chiang Ching often referred to her love of "luxuries." Yet
when her luxuries are identified, they seem trivial indeed:
rugs for her room, a fluorescent light that did not make a
humming sound, and "perfumed" air of the kind that we can
easily get in the United States with a dollar can of lemon
spray.

Of course there are some variations in the monotonous

patterns. Changchun, a city rebuilt after Japanese devastation, is a city of 240,000 workers and 1,000 factories, but it has tree-lined streets and parks that soften the effect of its look-alike housing blocks. The variety I found in Canton around the family courtyard reflects the city's earlier history (similar to Shanghai's) as home for wealthy merchants, mandarins, and foreign businessmen. But in New China, when adult children leave home for work assignments or to get married, other relatives usually move in to fill up the vacant beds. To my Chinese relatives, my parents live in quite wicked extravagance since their children moved out and left them in sole possession of a four-bedroom house.

It comes as a surprise to discover that a Communist country practices a form of segregated housing. Unlike the mixed races and occupations of an American apartment building, in China everyone is compartmentalized by jobs. One community in Shanghai houses only the 68,000 workers of a textile plant, for instance, and in Canton there is one building in which all the tenants work for the official China International Travel Service.

It seems strange, too, that in all the glowing accounts of life in the People's Republic of China and of happy workers in their look-alike apartments, most visitors do not recognize the biggest problem. For me, that problem was not the endless political speeches but the endless boredom.

Perhaps most of the "invited" travelers are kept so busy dashing in and out of model apartments and traveling to local farms or viewing archaeological marvels that they are too exhausted to notice or to care. My period as an "idle" relative gave me a different perspective.

Life in the PRC is built around group activity and public purpose. Sports, study, entertainment are all—like television watching—group affairs. The concept of free time in which to pursue one's own interests seems nonexistent. If accident or circumstance (such as mine) fails to keep your time programmed, what do you do?

That was why I was both delighted and surprised one evening when there was nothing officially planned; it was almost like an evening at home with my parents. As for the surprise, perhaps thanks are due to the return to power of Teng Hsiao-ping, a dedicated player, for I had always thought the game had a Western taint. . . . The last thing I would have expected in China was to sit down with my uncle and two aunts for a friendly game of bridge.

4

SUNDAY
IN THE PARK

TWELVE WEEKS in China—
two hours of talk. Only on Sunday and in a Canton park.

Everyone has a different tale to tell about finally making contact in the People's Republic of China, although some of the "contacts" are so predictable that they seem to have been scripted by official PRC publicity men. For me, perhaps traces of inhibitions from a Chinese-American upbringing created a barrier to intimacy, but whatever the reasons, there is a special pleasure in the moments when a mask slips and a stranger speaks.

After days and weeks of seeing only the surface—the smiling faces of enthusiastic workers, museum-tidy cement-floored barracks filled with model families, group performances of dam builders and gymnasts—some visitors might despair of ever having the kind of simple encounter that we take for granted at home. I was lucky. The family and I went to Yuehsiu Park.

Even Sunday has its group activities and planned programs in the PRC, but it is the one day when most people seem closest to a holiday mood. It is also a day that reminds those of us who live in America that happiness in China does not depend upon possessions—all the recreational vehicles and playthings of our familiar world.

Obviously no one goes for a Sunday drive in China. There are no private autos, and bicycles are mostly used for getting to work instead of for pleasure. Train excursions of the kind that I enjoyed in Europe and pleasure trips by bus are not part of the local picture. Any traveling done on a Sunday must be as purposeful as walking is on the weekday streets.

The people I saw going to the country for the day were not pleasure bound. Some were en route to work assignments. A sports team was traveling to an out-of-town match. A young woman was paying a once-a-year visit to her family. An engineer assigned to a remote provincial work site was arriving in Canton for his one-day-a-month visit with his wife and children. Only the Hong Kong departures and arrivals reminded me of the land of carefree travel beyond China's borders.

For their Sunday pleasure, my Canton relations go to the local park. Every town has its gardens and lakes, some built by volunteer labor. Many were once part of imperial palaces, or temples of Taoist mystics, or ancient moon-viewing pavilions. Some still have such traditional names as "Three Pools Mirroring the Moon" (in Hangchow) or "Dragon Light Pagoda." But it is impossible to escape such new-style names as "Park of Workers, Farmers, and Soldiers" or "Support-Agriculture Pond."

Setting out for Yuehsiu or Liuhua Park reminded me of going to San Francisco's Golden Gate Park when we were children, carrying picnic lunches and cameras. We were always excited about rowboats or pony rides, planning

Rowboats, a lake, a pagoda, a curved bridge: typical of China's many lovely parks. This is a scene from Canton's Liuhua.

to go on to the zoo later, hoping to ride on the merry-go-round. Yuehsiu and Liuhua do not have such exotic attractions as the marble boat built for an empress in one of Peking's parks, although Canton has its share of ancient buildings—including a pagoda more than a thousand years old, and the Chenhai (Zhenhai) Tower in Yuehsiu, built in 1380, and now a museum. There are monuments to modern history, too—especially the founder of modern China, Dr. Sun Yat-Sen—as well as a greater range of sports facilities, such as an enormous gym and an Olympic pool, than you find in most American parks.

The children at play, though, could have been in California. They were not playing baseball, a game that has not caught on in China. They were not throwing Frisbees or flying kites (in spite of the fact that kites are another Chinese invention). But some small boys were doing exactly what we used to do as third graders—playing a shoot-'em-up game with toy guns and rubber hand grenades, and yelling at the girls to keep away from their rocky fort. Two girls in red-and-white polka-dot dresses were hopscotching, their ribboned pigtails flying. A round-faced baby in a pram hugged a stuffed panda doll. Older boys practiced *t'ai chi*.

We found a nice quiet corner, where Granny and the aunties and uncles could sit. For backdrop, there was a fine display of flowers. All China's parks feature seasonal displays of azaleas, chrysanthemums, narcissus, and plum blossoms. It was a scene made for color, and I was soon snapping away. That was a mistake. Not because of a beady-eyed censor. The Chinese only object if you photograph wall posters (newspapers are "private"), or fancy a shot of "picturesque" buildings or people, because they think such old-fashioned scenes put China in a bad light.

The problem was replacing film. When I tried to buy more color, the answer was always: "We don't have any." Even black-and-white film was doled out one roll at a time. When I tried to stock up with half a dozen rolls to take with me to the commune, one of the other customers commented on "greedy" foreign tourists.

My few packs of Polaroid film were a great success. Handing out some of the prints, I made friends and even became an instant tourist attraction. Unfortunately, I realized too late that I had also seriously reduced the number of pictures I could take home. But it was worth it, to enjoy the unusual experience of voices speaking from conviction instead of from conditioning.

The young Hong Kong uncle, least-inhibited member of the family, strolled with me as I looked for candid shots. One young couple were waiting to have their picture taken by a public photographer—a regular feature of Chinese parks. Uncle Fong asked if his American nephew could take their picture, and after a bit of discussion they agreed. I peeled off the first print and offered it to them as a thank-you for posing. . . . And found I had taken a honeymoon souvenir!

Not all my married California friends took honeymoon trips—some seemed to prefer backpacking. But they all took at least a few days off from work. In modern China, however, the couples not only have no-frills ceremonies, in startling contrast to the old lavish celebration, they also go straight back to work on Monday morning. My couple would be back at lathe and spindle promptly at 6:30 A.M.

Children everywhere seem to be less inhibited than their elders. And it was the children in the park—away from the schoolyard and the group pressures that so often act as effective gags—who helped me to forget for a while that I too was now subject to the pressures of a family and must be careful not to "embarrass" them, for bureaucrats were sitting in judgment on my "capitalist-imperialist" behavior.

Some of the clustering children asked questions straight out of their geography classes: "Is there really gold in California?" "Do you grow two crops of rice in your home province?" I was even asked: "Who is looking after your pig while you are in China?" and "How many aqueducts have your workers built?" But when I tried to ask them questions, they giggled and fell silent.

One of the oddest discoveries for me was that the only American most of them knew by name was former President Nixon. And using the familiar term for an older person, one girl asked me: "How is Uncle Nixon now?"

We got some informal talk going when I produced some photos and showed them around—family pictures are

Undeterred by bad weather, the Chinese enjoy their city parks even on rainy days.

always a good beginning. But the photograph showing our four-bedroom house in the background proved a real puzzler. Everyone kept asking: "How many families live in these apartments?" Another puzzler was my Indian turquoise ring, a birthday present from my girl friend back home.

In China, birthdays are not celebrated. It was only after I returned home that I realized young Chen must have passed his thirteenth birthday without saying a word during the weeks that we shared a bedroom. Someone had told these children about another odd custom—double-ring wedding ceremonies. Even women do not wear wedding rings in China. No wonder that after a bit of nudging one of the girls came forward and asked me, "Where is your wife?"

We were collecting too big a crowd. Even Uncle Fong wanted to move along. And I was getting some strange looks from the public photographers. . . .

It had not occurred to me that I was interfering with a legitimate PRC worker. At home, everyone has his own equipment—Dad takes movies, Mother has her Instamatic, I play around with the latest through-the-lens gadgetry. At American tourist attractions, a public photographer is about as common as a dodo bird. In China, where cameras are 150-yuan luxury items and even my gift camera had limited use because of the family's film-buying problems, the public photographer is essential. Eager customers line up to get a souvenir of Granny at the Dragon Wall in Peking or of Mom and Dad marching through a once-restricted imperial archway.

A portrait or statue of Chairman Mao is a popular and politically correct backdrop (provided that you remember it is full-figure only, and mind you don't chop off his head). There is also an enormously popular picture of Mao and his successor Hua, titled: "With You in Charge,

The workers are inspired by large political posters, even in the parks beside the lovely displays of flowers.

I'm at Ease." Not everyone is at ease in their company, though.

One grandpa had got into several pictures where he was not a proper part of the scene. I have a whole series of photos marred by this old fellow staring into the camera or walking in front of a chattering group of grannies and blocking my view of a happy family. But when I tried to get him to pose in front of a Mao poster, he seemed to turn shy. I thought I heard him muttering to himself, "I'm not standing with that old brigand," as he hurried away to the refreshment stand.

Sometimes the park provided candid snapshots of another kind—scraps of overheard conversation, and even one brief family fight. Unlike the English, who drop their voices in public, the Chinese seem always to talk with the volume at full blast. Cousin Chen and I really upset the aunties later when we tuned in on these conversations and he started teaching me a few new Cantonese phrases. Mothers and aunts always do seem to put a stop to fun; and Auntie Chen kept reminding us that we were drawing too much attention to ourselves.

One family was squabbling about lunch. Until then I hadn't thought how funny it is that American families looking for an exotic meal eat a Chinese dinner, with chopsticks, while in Canton they go out for Italian spaghetti or German sausage—and half the fun comes from getting tangled up in those exotic instruments, a Western knife and fork. . . .

The family I was listening to had a megadecibel discussion going on about the relative merits of "the same old *dim sum*" and a much-too-expensive Western meal, eaten on a rooftop "where the Tangs went." At the height of the row, a guide shepherded a group of foreign tourists past— I suppose it was their "see the everyday life of the Chinese" segment. One asked, "What is that family arguing about?" Quick as a flash, the earnest tour guide claimed, "Chinese families do not argue. That is just the way spoken Chinese sounds. . . ."

When it came time for the family to eat, I found that —like some of Eileen's friends in Tokyo—if they say "We are going out for a picnic," what they really mean is "We are going to eat out." We went for *dim sum,* the "little jewels" I enjoy in California too, and the one meal that is designed to be a light refreshment, with plenty of tea and conversation on the side. The individual servings of two or three small steamed dumplings of pork (*shui-mai*) or shrimp (*har gow*), yam cakes, fried rice-dough balls puffed up and coated with sesame seeds, spring rolls (egg rolls) give you plenty of variety, without the stuffed feeling that always comes at the end of a banquet.

But I missed the familiar Western snacks—the hot dogs and French fries and take-away pizza slices. Here, there were only salted melon seeds or shredded dried plum to nibble on. And after five days of drinking nothing but tea, I didn't refuse the garishly colored local pop. It didn't taste quite as bad as it looked. Sugared sweet gourd on slivers of bamboo (a spring-festival specialty) was too sweet for my taste, and the local popsicles did not look very inviting. Ah, but the ice cream! The fried ice-cream balls were positively habit forming. And all the flavors were good—China's gift to European tables.

A snack counter in Chengtu offers a rich variety of fancy cakes to customers from six thirty in the morning until nine at night.

China News Service

Europe's gifts to China seem to have been in the field of sports, especially soccer. I tried to get into a lunch-time game a few times in Canton, and my lathe-operator friends (see Chapter 6) even invited me to join their basketball practice. I'd barely had time to shoot one basket when their coach came out. That was the end of my participation, and I received an explanation for the lack of friendly invitations from other groups I had watched. It seems that any team member who would "lose" five minutes of practice while an idler (outsider) played would be damaging his factory team's future chances of success.

But for its young people, modern China is a sportsman's heaven. They have everything—volleyball and basketball courts in the parks, huge soccer stadiums, places

Girls enjoy a game of badminton (foreground), while others get ready for basketball.

for hockey, tennis, even ice skating. The Chinese have loved sports for thousands of years—they had person-to-person combat and other games four thousand years ago. Unfortunately, no one seems to play just for fun. Everything involves competition—even work such as cabbage picking is turned into competitive sport. And everything is geared to the group, the facilities always described in terms of mass statistics. Peking's Workers' Stadium (built in 1962) seats 80,000; it has its own cafeteria, a movie theater, a hostel for 1,500 visiting athletes. I was terribly impressed by the massed drill teams in a Canton stadium that seats 30,000. But why is there so little pleasure taken in just playing the games?

Even badminton and table tennis are organized around interfactory matches and school rallies rather than private games. Track is a mass event, often with competing teams coming from all over the area. And no matter what the sport, the atmosphere tends to remind you of a high-school football game at home—complete with half-time drills.

These drills too are on an overwhelming scale, with hundreds of participants using colored shirts or scarves to make complicated Chinese ideographs. They do gym routines with hoops. I also discovered that in China jumping rope is not just a game for little girls in school playgrounds, or an exercise for boxers getting into shape for a match. It is a precision drill, with men and women lining up in cadenced leaps over a long, long rope.

This is also the country of the swimmer—a sport that seems to have been raised to the level of national myth. Chairman Mao wrote a famous poem called "Swimming" in June 1956—complete with references to Confucius ("the master"), and bits of old songs and legends along with the usual praises for young workers and modern flood-control projects. As you might expect with Mao, the poem also says that "Swimming is better far than idly strolling in a courtyard!"

Everyone insisted on telling me about Mao's famous swim across the Yangtze in 1966, when he was seventy-three years old. Ten years later, the memory was revived with a stamp issue. But for me, the most vivid memory of Chinese swimming was the odd scene at the huge pool, where instead of swimming nude, as we usually did in the college gym and at a favorite beach, we all had to climb into really gross black tank tops.

More disturbing was the fact that political messages intruded even in the swimming pool—and that political rallies often took over an otherwise tranquil park. Eileen had attended the May Day rally in Peking. Two thousand Little Red Guards ran to greet Chairman Hua as he extended "warm festival greetings," with much clapping and smiling from all concerned. The program included public readings of poetry, but not the lyrical recital once beloved of aristocrats. These were political messages in praise of PRC heroes and bitter attacks upon the current villains, the Gang of Four.

Sometimes an entire park will become a political center. In Shanghai, Eileen's relatives insisted that she visit the "rich man's house" where the Chinese Communist party was organized. She found that it had been turned into a national shrine, complete with souvenir postcards. In Canton, political parks ranged from those associated with the "colonial evils" of opium to those honoring the modern virtues of Mao and peasant education.

On later Sundays I found myself taking a course in modern Chinese history too, for Canton was the hometown of Dr. Sun Yat-sen. He founded the revolutionary "Revive China Society" in 1895, worked to overthrow the last imperial dynasty (the corrupt Manchu), and became first

President of the republic in 1912. Sun Yat-sen also founded the Kuomintang (National People's party)—a name that later unfortunately became associated with Chiang Kai-shek, just as Taiwan supporters have appropriated the festival of Double Ten in San Francisco.

One of Canton's parks honors the martyrs of the October 10 Battle of Canton (1911). Another commemorates the martyrs of the 1927 Canton Uprising. But when my cousins and I went to the Red Flower Garden, we were more interested in the refreshments and the rowboats than in the marble tomb of five thousand revolutionaries.

On that first Sunday in Canton, I had another view of politics-in-the-park—a simply super parade. What a show! It was a cross between an old-fashioned Fourth of July parade and a festival in San Francisco's Chinatown (although the Canton version lacked the traditional dragon dance).

To announce the theme, there were the traditional red banners, with ideographs lettered in white or gold. Children waved colored scarves. Rows of young workers were making a terrific noise with little brass cymbals, the size of Western castanets. Two boys pounded on a big drum of the kind used in China for centuries. Others played gongs and flutes just like those one might have heard in a temple courtyard a thousand years ago. To add to the noise, there were firecrackers—tossed underfoot or waved overhead, strung from long sticks.

If you have ever marched in support of Black Power, Peace in Vietnam, or the Save the Whale crusade, you notice a big difference between American parades and Chinese style marches. In China, marchers and onlookers alike were always on the same side. There were no demonstrations *against* a national policy. Rallies were always organized around government-sponsored themes, such as

"Support the National Conference on Learning from Taching in Industry," or "Support those who excel in political consciousness."

After hearing my father talk about some of the lovely old parks, I was disappointed with the present state of the thousand-year-old Temple of the Six Banyan Trees—but not too surprised that the family showed no interest in taking me to any of the other old memorials. They always seemed to have a reason to avoid these past scenes. Perhaps most are in disrepair or they are like the one my Hong Kong uncle claims is now used as a "warehouse" for surplus military equipment!

As a polite guest, I couldn't make my own requests about where we should go, so I was glad the family's plans included an introduction to Canton's night scene. Canton is lovely at night—especially if you look across from the far end of Haizhu Bridge at the bright lights of the twenty-seven-story Kwangchow Hotel and the tall buildings silhouetted against the sky. You can also watch the small boats, cargo-carrying barges, old-style sampans, and modern ferryboats, as they move along the Pearl River among reflected lights. Families walk along the riverbank, some on their way to the movies, or hurrying to do some after-work shopping or eating. Children are out late, too—usually on their way home from two hours of gym practice or rehearsals for a song recital.

Anyone accustomed to the United States—where to go into Central Park or Golden Gate Park after dark is to risk your life—is bound to be pleased with the freedom to stroll in Chinese parks at night. Anyone accustomed to a lively night on the town in New York or San Francisco, however, will probably be disappointed by the simple pleasures of a night on the town, Chinese style.

Canton's Cultural Park was different from anything I

had ever seen at home—a blend of carnival, concert hall, and Copenhagen's Tivoli—and I thoroughly enjoyed the experience. I was told that as many as fifty thousand people will be there on some festival nights. On other evenings, after I had sat through never-ending, dull political discussions, earnest revolutionary-literature classes, where I felt that I would never be "inside" my busy family's well-organized lives, it really felt good to stroll beneath the strings of colored lights and paper lanterns hanging from trees. There was an unbelievable range of things to do: the park had an aquarium, chess tables, exhibit halls, reading rooms, a shooting gallery—even an opera house and a ferris wheel.

The entrance to the Kwangchow Cultural Park.

The biggest crowds of all always seemed to gather around the open-air shows. And even a sudden rainstorm didn't stop the performance. I couldn't believe it: When the rain started, most of the audience stayed right where they were, and a volunteer jumped up on the stage to hold an umbrella over one of the actors—who went on posturing and jumping about the stage, unconcerned about damage to costume and makeup.

There was one group I could have watched forever— the acrobats. They were better than anything I had ever seen before. The Chinese acrobats seemed lighter than air, more like magicians than highly disciplined athletes. The show opened with a group of men and women and two small girls, all balancing and twirling on each other and on impossible towers and pyramids of chairs against a painted backdrop of mountains and fluffy white clouds.

A small girl rode out on a unicycle decorated with paper flowers; other girls twirled umbrellas and lengths of cloth in a pattern of red, white, and green. There were the usual tightrope walkers and trapeze artists. And then there were the jugglers! They tossed bowls of fire across the stage, balanced bowls filled with water, tossed a huge porcelain jar back and forth between heads and feet as though it were a rubber ball. A woman balanced on a ladder while she twirled uncountable numbers of rings. There were also routines with twirling bamboo poles, with ancient broadswords, and a strongman exerting a 400-kilogram force to bend five long bows. A boy went diving through a hoop.

I had heard about these acrobats, whose existence can be traced back to 200 B.C., when groups using props from everyday life traveled about the country. In the past they used to be regarded as vagabonds but in the New China their skills have been elevated to a national art form and troupes are even sent abroad to perform. Sometimes, too,

Canton's own acrobatic troupes perform regularly and include a group of child performers. A typical audience includes workers of all ages.

like other artists in the PRC, they travel about the country, working for a full day at factory or coal mine and then putting on a show after dark.

The acrobats use some motifs rarely encountered in modern China. We watched a lion with long golden hair, green topknot, a huge red mouth. On the lion's back, a baby "lion" juggled a huge colored ball. A girl leaped onto the back of the lion, two lion-costumed acrobats jumped to her shoulders, somersaulting and leaping from one ball to another and onto a teeter-totter balanced on yet another huge ball.

Jostled by the crowd, we continued to wander among outdoor stages—where, as usual, a concert featured the concerto "Battling the Typhoon." Most of the musical offerings didn't hold my attention. Western music and Chinese classics alike seemed to be nonexistent in 1977, although I heard about an all-Beethoven concert in Peking. But since 1978 the repertoire once again includes the music of Western composers, as well as ancient folk songs, and even *The Tale of the White Snake,* a musical setting of a centuries-old Chinese love story. When I was in Canton, however, traditional Chinese tunes that my father plays on the flute and the folk songs my mother taught me seemed to have vanished, to be replaced by new operas and folk tunes —all with near-identical themes.

Ballet, folk dances, puppet shows, song recitals—even comic acts—all seemed to have titles such as "Carrying Manure" or "Brother and Sister Reclaim the Wasteland." If you don't happen to be caught up in Communist ideology, it is hard to enjoy a group of patriotic poets crying: "Liberate Taiwan!" or to get involved in a dance-drama showing "Shanghai Against the Imperialists."

According to one of the cousins, some of the jokes in the skits we saw were quite hostile to the "Western imperialists." But although Eileen said she had heard of an exhibition of political cartoons in Shanghai, I did not see anything that expressed political criticism of Mao's and Hua's regimes. The attacks were all reserved for groups and individuals (like the Gang of Four), who had been officially declared enemies. Only once did I hear even cranky old Uncle Wang troubled by a political joke—he seemed to detect "dangerous" political thinking in an allusion to some local official. But that allusion and most of the jokes were entirely too subtle for my Westernized ears.

Perhaps I was lucky that I did not understand. Sometimes in the PRC I wondered if *lack* of understanding was the real key to enjoyment. It is easy for those enthusiastic foreign visitors to talk about "gorgeous" colors and the "graceful" movements of "impressive" spectacles when they are ignorant of the old melodies, when they know

Girl with Chinese four-stringed lute (*p'i p'a*). This instrument has been used since the T'ang dynasty (618–906 A.D.), sometimes for solos, often to accompany storytelling.

nothing of the way in which an old folk theme had been debased for use in tiresome political education.

Only the acrobats and the performing animals seem to escape the tainting of entertainment with message. The clowns, conjurer, and talking parrot might all have stepped out of a small-town circus tent in America. At the zoo, foreign visitors and party officials alike laughed at the cat-bears (pandas)—one lying on his back, another rolling about, a third happily nibbling on a branch, and all blissfully unaware of the world of hard work and stern political messages. . . .

5

ABACUS, BRUSH, AND LITTLE RED BOOK

AT HOME in California, visiting school classrooms does not come high on my entertainment list, even during annual Open House. Going back to school in Canton was different, rather like going behind the scenes at the circus to see how the highly disciplined performers learn to do their stunts. I was very curious to see how a lively small cousin such as Chen could be transformed into one of those owlish young technicians more interested in studying Mao "On Contradiction" than in studying girls or football scores.

Before I stepped through the doorway with young Chen, one of the other cousins provided a briefing. It all sounded suspiciously like heaven: no grades and no exams; textbooks written by students, teachers disciplined by their students at school assemblies ("criticism time"); the only report cards those written by a visiting factory committee, grading not the students but their teachers.

Everything sounded ideal, with a relevant curriculum

consciously geared to current events, and instead of busy-work shop classes, a genuine minifactory in which the twelve-year-olds assemble electronic circuits and even second graders produce chess sets and school furniture. I was told no one has to sweat over abstruse theories: physics lessons get practical application in the making of electrical fans. And sometimes the students go out into the real world, to get their factory experience at the lathes of a neighbor-hood plant.

My first close-up view of this up-to-date utopia was a mind-boggling survival from the past. I have often seen old herbalists in Chinatown totting up abacus beads with diz-zying speed. It is quite different to watch the abacus used

Even on the coolest days of winter, the children wear gay colors and prints.

side by side with new computer gadgetry. It was disturbing, too, to watch the eight-year-olds doing lightning-quick abacus calculations up to ten thousand in the time it took me to add up to one hundred. It was even more disturbing to think about some of the modern uses of this "quaint" old counting device—creating China's atom bomb in 1964, for instance, the H-bomb in 1967, the sophisticated satellites since 1970.

But the most disturbing moment of the day came when my cousin—so lively at home and in the park—suddenly seemed to be transformed into an ideologically correct young robot. Perhaps his mechanical performance in the classroom was related to the presence of a foreign cousin.

Inside a typical Canton classroom. Portraits of the late Chairman Mao and Chairman Hua look down on the students in a middle-school physics class.

. . . Yet here was Chen—who never uses "group-speak" at home, who lives in a household where the only political speeches are occasional harangues on the radio—standing up with his class to chant "I love Chairman Mao" routines.

Visitors who tell of classes where Chairman Mao's *Little Red Book* serves as all-purpose text, however, must be quoting from out-of-date magazine stories. There are far fewer copies of the book that once served as primer for adult literacy classes and first-grade readers alike. Not that Mao and his thoughts have vanished from the scene since his death!

Cousin Chen's classroom has a huge portrait of Mao, with calligraphy brush in hand, writing the much-quoted text: "China's future belongs to You!" ("Young people are full of vigor . . . like the sun at eight or nine in the morning. . . . China's future belongs to you.") Another classroom displayed student calligraphy—endless repetitions of a banner headline, "Eternal Glory to the Great Leader and Great Teacher, Chairman Mao Tse-tung."

Mao's vision of himself as national teacher (his profession before he took up revolution as a way of life) has in fact so formed the attitudes expressed everywhere today that I was glad one of my professors had recommended that I look at the *Little Red Book* for a bit of pre-China conditioning. My sister the teacher approves of some of Mao's statements on education, such as its purpose: "To enable everyone to develop morally, intellectually, and socially." Western theories of open universities seem to be anticipated in his early recommendation of a "self-study university" (in 1921, when most Chinese were lucky to complete a few primary grades), studying independently, as he himself had done. Many California schools agree with Mao's "Knowledge Begins with Practice."

Yet even before you enter a Chinese classroom, there

are hints of the odd ways in which Mao's theories have been applied. Like a properly canonized saint, Mao is continually given credit for miraculous cures and achievements. Workers cite his 1937 essays "On Practice" and "On Contradiction" in circumstances where one would have thought technical education more appropriate than Mao's "inspiration"—development of the Taching Oil Field, basic mathematics research, construction of a 960-channel microwave communications system.

After such heady stuff, it was a relief to find that students still get a good dose of basics in the classroom, right from their first day at the age of seven, until they graduate from middle school six or seven years later. The supposedly easy schools demand some very hard work.

Chen's school resembled its American counterparts in size: 3,500 students and 180 teachers. The subjects he studies have the familiar names: language, literature, mathematics, music, physical education, science. But he also studies Mao thought, as well as the theories of Lenin and Marx, takes classes in military training, and puts in several hours each week at "productive labor" (some factory or agricultural work that is always coordinated with more conventional classwork). His school day runs from 7:30 A.M. to 3:40 P.M. six days a week, although there are local and seasonal variations throughout the country. There are breaks in the day, but these are often spent tending the schoolyard vegetable patch or getting in some extra sports practice.

Going from class to class, I made a discovery: the subjects might be called by familiar names, but the content was radically different, and the differences could not all be blamed on Communist ideology. Writing, for instance. I had been proud to master one hundred ideographs in San Francisco, yet when Chen's teacher invited me to write my name on the board, my clumsy strokes provoked consider-able laughter. Imagine a great big foreign cousin writing like a first grader!

Each ideograph is made up of a number of basic strokes, and these must always be written in the same order: horizontal —, vertical 十, middle stroke 丨 before the two sides 小, and so on. Some characters require only a few strokes (two for "person," 人, three for "big," 大 four for "fire," 火). Others have more than twenty.

No wonder that even in the modern PRC, people take pride in their calligraphy, just as scholars did long ago. In Chinese literature courses in San Francisco, students read

A student displays his skill in the difficult art of callig-raphy.

the classic verses of Po Chü-yi (A.D. 772 to 846). In the PRC, the calligraphy of such ancient poets and scholars gets low marks. Popular works today have titles such as "I Sing of Anshan Steel" or "The Lamp in Premier Chou's Office." Verses written by political and military heroes are especially prized. Even a movie can be given a stamp of approval with a caption written "in Chairman Mao's very own calligraphy."

Sometimes the beauty of calligraphy leads to funny misunderstandings by (illiterate) Westerners. I still remember the friend visiting Hong Kong just before the 1970's diplomatic thaw, who had been pleased with a gift of "lovely Chinese calligraphy." That gift was not quite so well received when my father translated: "Long live the Great People's Republic of China," "We passionately love Chairman Mao," and finally, "Down with Nixon!"

Seeing at first hand the problems involved in mastering calligraphy, I began to have a better understanding of my father's continual nagging about schoolwork. No wonder that he was always telling me I was lazy and that students worked harder in China. Even learning to read is terribly hard, and using a dictionary seems like a task beyond anyone but the most sharp-eyed detective.

Instead of our alphabetical listing in twenty-six-letter sequence, there are forty thousand or so characters, arranged according to more than two hundred classifiers (radicals). To read a newspaper you need to know a thousand ideographs. To read simple books, my father uses more than three thousand; for the classics, ten times as many.

Few people in China seemed to be reading those classics in 1977. Looking in bookshops and on the shelves of my Canton family, I saw few of the volumes my father enjoys. Whenever I referred to one of the authors that he

Two students practice speedy calculations on the abacus. When not in use, each abacus hangs by a permanent cord attached to the back of the desk.

quotes, or that I had read in translation at school, I just got blank looks from the younger cousins and uncles, although they could quote from Mao's essays. It also sounded as if

Chen's study of "revolutionary history" were teaching him that the world sprang full-grown from the inspired brush of Chairman Mao.

Chen and his classmates recited all the details of Mao's Long March. But they knew little of the earlier dynasties and settlements. They could list all the modern monuments, but could not identify the settlement that existed in the area of present-day Peking four thousand years ago, or the city named Peiping (perhaps because that was Chiang Kai-shek's name for the city during the period 1928–1930). In 1976 Eileen found that even students in college history and literature classes were relentlessly contemporary. They seemed to ignore fifteen-hundred-year-old manuscripts in the university library, ancient philosophers, twelfth-century collections of poetry. They were reading Mao's essays, texts of some modern "revolutionary operas," and precisely one story by the modern novelist Lu Hsün (Xun).

Yet translations of Lu Hsün and other moderns provided my first glimpses of the realities of my father's homeland. It was in their pages that I began to understand the conditions that led to the revolution. Poor Chen was even denied the pleasure of laughing at *Flowers in the Mirror,* in which a traveler rather like Gulliver is lost in "the country of women"—where the role-reversal includes ladies bathing him, braiding his hair, and decking him with lipstick and jewels.

Some of Chen's books were attractive to look at, printed in easy-to-read characters and clear primary colors, with serial pictures (rather like comic books) for the youngest ones. But the books were all overburdened with PRC ideas. The heroes and heroines were all earnest types devoted to Good (Communist or revolutionary) Works— usually in a tone that reminded me of Sunday-school texts.

The Chinese eliminate the Almighty, but the message remains, "Do good unto thy neighbor."

Good little PRC "soldiers" learn that "helping others is a pleasure." Junior offers Granny his magnet to help her find a needle. The good little girl takes an extra sweater to school, to lend to the friend whose working mother will not have heard the weather forecast of icy-cold winds. Travelers on a long-distance train gladly sacrifice their personal needs (they even remain docilely aboard for several hundred kilometers beyond their destinations) in order to carry a wounded Five-Good Soldier to a distant hospital. A Five-Good Soldier is an idealized soldier whose life purportedly exemplifies "five goods"—good political work, good ideological work, good working style, good military training, and good conduct in everyday life.

With such conditioning, no wonder that so many reports on modern China sound so suspiciously alike, the everyday actions of so many citizens so unbelievably virtuous and self-effacing. As far as I could see, the conditioning goes right down to the kindergarten we passed on the way to my cousin's classroom. The art project, an exercise in paper cutting, was a large Red Star.

In the first-grade classrooms of the school, I saw children playing with blocks—as they do the world over. Their project? A miniature Tien An Men, so that they could be-enact the annual military review and parade of the October 1 national holiday. In French class, children really were reciting, *"J'aime Président Hua,"* although I had thought that was an invention of roving reporters. Music classes included the classical flutes and two-stringed violin (*erh-hu*) as well as Western instruments (all owned by the school), but like the performers in the park they were playing "Sending Fertilizer to the Fields."

The few fragments of traditional Chinese arts that I

A school orchestra prepares to play for a group of visitors.

did see were as scarce as gold coins. First graders were performing "galloping horses" and a ribbon dance that my sisters had learned in Chinatown classes. I also watched boys and girls performing the traditional martial arts (*wu shu*), just as their ancestors had fenced with rods and broadswords, practiced archery, *kung fu,* and *t'ai chi* in earlier centuries.

It didn't take me long to spot some of the flaws in what I had thought of as a good school system. The absence of grade pressures sounded fine until I sat in on a middle-school session of criticism and found three pious little beasts attacking a soft-voiced older teacher—not for her academic or social shortcomings but for having "a bad political attitude." Having no final exams sounded like heaven— until I got to talking with one of the teachers, who patiently explained that *of course* students (in higher grades and in college at least) are always evaluated by a (Communist) party committee. Similarly, the "good" practical mini-factories that I thought would be so much more interesting than the shop classes I had taken had to be balanced against a school program in which the students actually have no choices at all.

All my life I have been able to make choices. I cannot imagine schools without electives. Nor can I imagine schools without special classes for slow learners and for gifted students. When I asked Chen's teacher about special classes, he appeared to be scandalized. Surely I knew that the girl who had difficulty with the classwork was the victim of bad teaching methods only? When a student is what we would call a slow learner, each of the other members of the class works with him, until the slow learner raises his hand to indicate, "I understand."

What about gifted students? The answer was a stern "We have no education for geniuses here." After all, every graduate of middle school would go straight into the labor force (see Chapter 6) for a minimum of two years. In 1978, however, the Chinese began to set up special "key" schools for gifted students.

Eileen and I had both been eager to see what the open-to-all Chinese universities are like. We were both disappointed.

In theory, anyone can go to college. There are no college-prep courses, no academic prerequisites, no qualifying exams. We were told there was only one requirement —those two years of full-time "productive labor" after the fourteen-year-old student graduates from middle school. No one is denied a college place for lack of money, we were told. The university charges no fees and provides subsistence allowances (full salary for some workers). Secondary education was not an essential halfway step. A 1976 stamp issue summed it up: "Workers, peasants, and soldiers go to university."

But I got so many excuses when I tried to see these wonderful university students for myself that I was ready to give up. It wasn't until I agreed to go with one of the Travel Service cousin's groups that I finally met a live freshman class. The student body didn't look much like a college class at home, where more than 90 percent of the freshmen are obviously just out of high school.

The group included a forty-five-year-old coal miner, several middle-aged factory workers, and a woman who claimed to be a former slave. I began to suspect that the ever-present slave figure was a plant (suspiciously like the one described in the border-station literature), until I got home and Eileen told me about a document she had seen in Peking.

The document recorded the sale of a female slave less than forty years ago. It had been "sealed" by the girl's father, as well as by village officials and her new owner. Of course, such papers can be faked, but it looked very authentic with its various red "chops" (the vermilion-ink seals used by the Chinese to authenticate documents, comparable to our notary public's seal). So, slavery did exist in Old China, and perhaps was so widespread that the ever-present "former slave" was genuine.

Other students had come from a commune, their only preparation a year of primary school. One was even battling what I should have regarded as an impossible handicap—"preparation" that consisted entirely of one literacy crash course, after fifteen years of operating a cotton loom.

But as I had already suspected from listening in while I roamed the streets of Canton, frank discussion with these students seemed next to impossible. The official group I was with (and Eileen's unofficial visits in Shanghai and Peking) included "question-and-answer" sessions. But the responses were only self-conscious stock answers—even when party watchdogs were not listening in. There seemed to be a self-imposed censorship operating—a reticence even more pronounced than the usual holding back of responses to strangers. On the other hand, many of the students seemed to share a truly passionate belief in China's new-style education.

It is difficult for a visitor like me to judge just how good—or bad—the quality of college courses has become. European and American professors who visited classes during the mid-seventies do not all agree about the level of instruction or even the content of classes. I myself did not see anything that corresponded to our Western humanities courses. My cousins were not taking a course entitled "History of Chinese Civilization," for instance. I later learned, however, that a number of the classics (both Chinese and Western), which had not been readily available for twenty years in some cases, suddenly reappeared in the bookstores toward the end of 1977. These volumes included the *Odes of the Sung Dynasty*, Li Po's eighth-century poems, Lu Hsün's modern novels, and works by Balzac, Defoe, De Maupassant, Dickens, Shakespeare, and Mark Twain in translation.

The authorities announced that there would be less time spent on political study and more on advanced scientific theory. But that did not indicate the rehabilitation of ancient philosophy, especially Confucianism. Various campaigns against the privileges of the old intellectual elite or mandarins (reaffirmed during the Cultural Revolution) have made sure of that. For college students, however, there will definitely be less time spent in workshops and more time spent working on scientific theory. China's proud tradition of centuries of scientific invention will thus be restored and maintained.

During my visit, I found the answers to specific questions about admission procedures disappointing. The "open" university did not open its doors in response to the knocking of individual students. One or two of the freshman class said that there had been a notice on the factory bulletin board, and they had submitted or volunteered their names to be considered for two university places. They had ultimately been chosen by the factory's selection committee, as had other students in that class.

The decision-by-committee system so prevalent in China operates first at the place of work (selection of possible students). Then a local (Communist) party committee goes over the applicants, eliminating any who show signs of selfish motives. Finally, an interviewing team from the college talks to the candidate, occasionally arranging for deferred enrollment if the local quota has been filled.

If a university has several openings in the mathematics department or a technical college has openings in livestock management, "fellow workers" (that is, committees) select candidates whose job skills might be improved by such training, or who could contribute more to the commune or coal mine or industrial plant as a result of additional study. Usually, the students expect to return to their jobs right after training and to apply their new expertise in the same factory or farm operation that they had left two or three years earlier.

Exams for entrance and for college graduation were temporarily eliminated in the early 1970's, replaced by such awful alternatives as a test of political attitude and "revolutionary" consciousness. The criteria for selection still have little basis in personal motives or individual talents in most cases. The one essential is group need.

Just what goes on in the classrooms at the moment is a subject of debate among more expert observers than I am. Even Eileen's college-professor father says that it is impossible to tell. And I was not the only visitor thwarted in attempts to do some informal sitting in on regular university classes. Some of the difficulties resulted from the Cultural Revolution of the summer of 1966—events that make the unrest on college campuses in Europe, Japan, or the United States seem like children's pranks by comparison.

Chinese students were political activists long before their Western counterparts. They rebelled against their curriculum back on May 4, 1919, for instance. At that time, they protested against the old authoritarian "abuses by family, school, and state." Again in 1966, students were the active instruments of drastic political change.

In the summer of 1966, the first Big Character posters, huge notices listing a person's "crimes" for all to see, were put up at Peking University. They severely criticized various officials. A week later, Chairman Mao ordered a radio broadcast declaring the Cultural Revolution as party policy, and identifying its sixteen points. The Red Guards organized—first in the universities, but later joined by middle-school students. Often they became physically violent in their enthusiasm for "getting rid of the past" or "sweeping away old cultural objects." Their verbal attacks included such phrases as "the basic truths of Marxism-Leninism" (truths they said had been neglected by the officials they criticized), and an outcry against "the corruption of people by bourgeois movies" (or books or plays).

Work at the lathe: an experience that begins in middle school.

The political upheaval covered by the Cultural Revolution eventually got so out of hand that the party officials had a hard time restoring discipline. In many cases, overzealous young revolutionaries had already destroyed art treasures and buildings that could not be replaced. No wonder that the situation in universities has been so confused. Classes were suspended on October 26, 1966, and many universities and secondary schools remained closed until 1970 or later. In 1971, fewer than half of the college classes had been restored. Many universities had changed into unrecognizable forms. Everyone seemed to be majoring in political or revolutionary studies. One of Eileen's

Shanghai cousins said that they spent more time criticizing the content of courses and the political thinking of their teachers than in studying such announced topics as theoretical physics.

When the universities began to reopen in 1970, many of the professors had vanished (at least temporarily)— sent to remote areas to be "re-educated" through such tasks as tending camels, stamping out machinery parts, and shoveling manure. No one was too grand for this humbling re-education, and college discussion leaders were forever citing such examples as the famous Dr. Lin Chiao-chi (also known as Dr. Khati Lim), a gynecologist and obstetrician of international reputation, who was head of her department at the Capital Hospital in Peking. When her turn came for re-education, she found herself face to face with "ordinary" Chinese people for the first time in her life. Her self-criticism has been widely published and quoted, especially the line "I cure their physical ills, while they cure my sick thinking."

Such re-education was a comparatively mild treatment. Japanese professors whose papers were burned or American teachers whose classes were boycotted in the 1960's had an easy time in comparison with the Chinese professors, who were often attacked with physical violence —although the favorite weapon of attack was the Big Character poster.

The teachers' "crimes" listed on the posters seem both petty and incomprehensible to many Western visitors. Often the students simply attacked a professor on obscure points of Chinese Communist doctrine. Or the poster might accuse a teacher of failure to "adhere to the party's basic line." Such an accusation was often triggered by the teacher's insistence on maintaining high academic standards or setting examinations. Students faced with a tough exam might write on the paper "This is a bourgeois trick!" and this "brilliant criticism" might well result in the teacher's being sent away for "re-education." In this period, the bad guys were the "intellectuals," teachers who preferred study and theory to practice.

Big Character posters are also used to correct the errors of supervisors in industry, and even party leaders are not immune. The ultimate example is the attack on the Gang of Four—Chang Chun-shiao, Wang Hung-wen, Yao Wen-yuan, and Mao's widow Chiang Ching. Chiang Ching had been the leader in the censorship of books, films, and plays, even trying to ban the film *Pioneers* (the story of the Taching oilfield) in mid-1975—although Chairman Mao thwarted that attempt, calling their actions "nitpicking." She and her friends also tried to suppress the film made on the death of Premier Chou En-lai, showing the crowds mourning throughout China—a continuation of earlier attempts to discredit and oust Chou.

The Gang's attacks on political leaders, writers, film-makers, artists, and musicians were made with familiar words of political rhetoric. Now they themselves are criticized for practicing revisionism, for worshiping things foreign, and for suppressing or tampering with Chairman Mao's directives, as well as sabotaging the Cultural Revolution and undermining those twin glories, Taching and Tachai. Items in Chinese newspapers say that earlier articles praising the Gang's role in art and literature were written or specially commissioned by Chiang Ching and her friends.

A thirty-five-year-old student at the Conservatory of the May 7 University of Arts in Peking is given credit for putting up the Big Character posters that heralded the Gang's ouster. He was imprisoned for 108 days and only released when the Gang members were arrested themselves on October 6, 1976. Later developments included a campaign led by the new chairman, Hua: "Expose and Criticize the Gang of Four" (who have since been blamed not only for the state of literature and art, but also for economic sabotage, labor troubles at Nanchang Tractor Plant, and any otherwise hard-to-understand falling off of production figures).

I wish that I had been able to spend some time in one of the May 7 schools—part of Mao's plan to "turn all of China into one great school"—especially while the student body was largely made up of formerly elite civil servants and intellectuals who had been sentenced to rural "re-education." I did meet one graduate of the program in Kwangtung Province—not a credit to the system, I'm afraid. In fact, he was still shockingly outspoken (quite unlike my peaceable Canton connections).

When we met he was using abacus and pen to keep the production team's accounts. Formerly a professor of advanced mathematics, he had been "sent down" to the country to be taught more humble attitudes, beginning with the point that rice is not just a readily available food to be eaten with chopsticks out of his (aristocratic) porcelain bowl. He was made to follow the full cycle: getting out in the mud, planting, tending, harvesting, threshing. Such labor was supposed to add a sweet new proletarian flavor to the old staple rice bowl. In his case, the professor said, "It was a bitter waste of time."

The supply of recalcitrant professors for May 7 schools began to dwindle. Most declared themselves suitably reformed after a few months in the country. Like tortured spies in wartime, they would confess to anything—although, like double agents, they were usually more careful to conceal their true thoughts from curious travelers like me.

As far as I could see, the May 7 schools now concentrate on technological training. In remote areas, former herdsmen are brought into similar technical schools and transformed into doctors, teachers, or statisticians. There is even a kind of quota system operating here. For instance, the graduates are geared to such communal needs as a carefully calculated two electricians per brigade. Sometimes, a whole industry becomes a school. At Changchun, 10,000 technicians have been trained at the auto plant and sent out as teacher-workers. Taching has served as a practical lab for the training of 56,000 oilfield personnel.

Eileen's experiences in Peking were more varied than mine, because of her father's studies at the prestigious Peking University and his continued correspondence with some faculty members. She knew that even while the university was closed, important work had continued—for instance, at the Institute of Mathematics of the Chinese Academy of Sciences, with advanced research in distribution theory. Yet much of the campus at Peking University had been transformed into a sort of industrial town, with a workshop making pharmaceuticals, an electronics assembly line, and so on.

This confusion between universities and factories seemed wasteful. We went with friends to try to sit in on university classes, and invariably we found ourselves steered instead to the college "shop," where the students with whom we had hoped to talk about university life were busy putting together circuitry or bottling pills. At the Provincial Teachers College in Kwangtung Province, they were making radio amplifiers and research oscilloscopes. Eileen went onto one campus where the college buildings were still under construction. It turned out that the "construction workers" were students and teachers, who were quite literally building their school from the ground up.

There was only one school in all of China that we

really admired, the Central Institute for Nationalities in Peking. When Eileen visited it, she saw seven hundred students from forty-six national groups, many of whom had been very hostile to one another in the past. They were wearing national dress—Pai girls in brilliant red jumpers, Yi women in rainbow-striped skirts—very different from the drab muffled-up figures in heavy jackets and ear-flapped hats out on Peking's winter streets (where the temperature was about −4° Celsius). In order to bring these non-Han students into the mainstream of Chinese life, they study the common speech (*putonghua*), and then go on to such advanced scientific studies as genetics research and satellite engineering, or subjects related to their pastoral homelands. At the same time these students were learning about their own cultural heritage. There is no discrimination against

Mongolian herdsman and his family.
China News Service

"minority peoples" in modern China. On the contrary, they are honored, and their special heritage is displayed and explained at the Nationalities Cultural Palace.

This interest in other Chinese cultures did not extend to an interest in cultures outside the PRC. Apart from the eager children in the park, no one wanted to know anything about my life in the United States, and no one asked Eileen about her everyday experiences in Japan and Canada. There seemed to be few international exchange students (with the exception of some "friends of China" political appointees). Even the students at Peking Language Institute—who were learning English, French, German, Arabic, and Spanish (in that order of enrollment)—were all there as the result of on-the-job needs, not personal choice. They were destined to go overseas in the service of Chinese technology, or to act as interpreters for diplomats, cultural emissaries, and foreigners touring along the official China Travel Service routes.

A few of the teachers Eileen and I met talked darkly about the breakdown of educational standards and lower quality of work—many of the same concerns of parents and teachers in the United States. None of the teachers seemed worried that little Chen or young Wang couldn't read, at least—they are secure in the strong program of basics. But some shared my father's traditional feeling about the importance of intellectual discipline. As one said, "Sending the best brains to grow vegetables in the country will result in squash-heads in university classes."

One of the old professors who had been at school with Eileen's father even said, "Too many people have forgotten that there is no correlation between good Communist conduct and advanced mathematics or physics." Perhaps that old professor demonstrates the traditional Chinese belief that the elders always know best. A few months after I returned home, American papers began to carry reports about the bad effects of too much "practice" and too little theory in Chinese education. By the end of 1977, some universities had acknowledged that students spending too much time on college assembly lines lacked the essential theory for doing advanced scientific research. A few schools had almost returned to the tough standards of the days before the Cultural Revolution.

Eileen and I both feel that our questions about Chinese education cannot really be answered yet. There have been so many changes in the schools of China—especially in the colleges and at the secondary level—that what one sees one year may be drastically altered by the next.

Friends who visited the Peoples Republic of China in 1978 found that the average age of the freshman class at Tsinghua University was 20.2 years. These students entering college in February (the beginning of the academic year in China) had an average grade of 82 in politics, mathematics, language, physics, and chemistry—information that was included in newspaper reports from the PRC as evidence of new educational policies under the new leadership.

Before the Cultural Revolution, students progressed through upper middle school directly to college. After that, it was almost impossible to find anyone who had skipped the essential "two years hard labor" as a prerequisite for university entrance—although my Hong Kong uncle claimed to have friends who had managed it.

In Canton, I met two or three people in their twenties who laughed when I asked about their experiences as commune workers. "Commune work? Working in the fields? I did a bit of part-time agriculture in middle school, but I went straight on to five years of college after that!" Nobody imagined in 1977, however, that a year later 20 percent of entering college students would be coming directly from such middle schools, usually after two or three years in "upper" middle school.

Committees still determine just who shall go to college, but in contrast to the teachers who were shocked at my references to "gifted" students, a government directive now specifies that "outstanding students" may go straight from middle school to university (although anyone expecting to return to farm work is supposed to attend agricultural college instead). After eleven years without formal entrance requirements, college-entrance exams have been restored. Standards of professional education are also returning to their earlier high levels. The vice-president of the Chinese Academy of Sciences has outlined plans for a nationwide research program in science and technology by 1985.

Perhaps that program—like the programs started after the Cultural Revolution—will in turn be replaced by officially sanctioned new policies in 1985. But at the moment, official statements say that 70 percent of the students at Peking University are the children of workers, peasants, and even "revolutionary intellectuals," while others are "young compatriots from Taiwan, Hong Kong, and Macao," and "returning young Chinese from abroad." Who knows, perhaps some of my California cousins will be able to attend college classes with their relatives in Kwangtung Province soon. Young Chen has just missed the benefits of the new policy. He had to serve his two years of hard labor first.

6

SOLDIER, SHIPBUILDER, STATISTICIAN

GOING TO WORK at fourteen strikes most American students as a hardship, although in many other parts of the world it is commonplace. Most of my older aunts and uncles still remember the old days in China, when children of eight or nine years old were sent out to work in Kwangtung's fields—often under conditions that I thought had ended about the time of Europe's Middle Ages.

Some of my California friends say that they would rather go to work at fourteen than go to school. But for me, the lack of choice in China—whether or not I could go to college and what kind of work I could do—would be intolerable. My first reaction to the work scene in Canton was that I must be back in grammar school, where teachers were forever saying, "Do as you're told!"

Talking to my cousins, though, I began to realize that if you have grown up under the Chinese system of organization and committees, it does not seem nearly as confining as it does to outsiders. In fact, my Chinese relations regard my infinite choices as confusing and too "selfish" for their taste.

Young Chen would have had plenty of work experience before his graduation, including all those hours of "productive labor" ever since he was a first grader. He was looking forward to his final school year, when the entire class would spend two months at a rural branch school, studying for two thirds of each day, joining other commune workers out in the fields for the rest of the time. He and his friends—like thirteen-year-olds in other countries—were rather pleased at the thought of being away from their families for a while. They also looked forward to the fringe benefits—meeting country cousins they would otherwise never see, and traveling outside Canton (which they could otherwise do only if they had received special permission).

One day I asked some of these thirteen-year-olds the simple question "What would you like to do after rural school?" You would have thought that I had switched from Cantonese to Swahili. What would "liking" or "wanting" have to do with their work assignments? To the average Western visitor, their stock answers sound rehearsed: "I shall go where I am needed, of course."

The answer is sincere. None of these boys and girls has any experience in making personal choices. Pressing for answers, I had to rephrase the question. Then one girl answered, "Well, I have a cousin in the People's Liberation Army." Young Tien-ming listed the occupations of his relatives: "Uncle Li is a doctor. Auntie Fang's brother works at the Shanghai Shipyard. My elder sister does research for a brigade in the Nei Mongol [Inner Mongolia] Autonomous Region." Other students identified brothers and sisters and cousins in every imaginable occupation from unskilled hotel worker to statistician in a government laboratory.

One entire class of the previous year's graduates had been sent directly from school to join a commune's work teams. I tried to imagine thirty-five Cleveland students being sent en masse to labor in the Nebraskan wheat fields or twenty New Yorkers shipped off to herd sheep among the sagebrush of Nevada.

In China, such assignments are commonplace. Ten million "educated young people" have been sent to rural areas in the past ten years—to help reclaim the Gobi desert, to labor in Taching's oilfields, or to transform wastelands into apple orchards, fish-filled lakes, and cornfields. But just as summer work camps bore some American students, Chinese boys and girls often tire of farm work and want to return to the city scene after the novelty of a few weeks in the country wears off. In theory, the minirebels are cured by a program of "re-education" that includes the inspiration provided by tales of the hardships experienced by farmers and other workers in the past. Perhaps the system works, but most of the tales of re-education that I heard were unverified and second hand.

Friends back in California say that they would not mind volunteering for remote adventures—research at the South Pole or mining in Alaska, for example. They think it would be more fun than the standard curriculum of colonial history or the plays of Shakespeare. I am not so sure. Most of China's "productive" labor assignments sound more like a life sentence at hard labor to me.

Only one form of student labor sounded really attractive (at least to begin with)—working on the railroad. The Children's Railway in Harbin has nothing in common with familiar Western amusement-park rides. It is a well-run commercial operation, technically correct in every de-

Working on the railroad that runs from the border to Canton and beyond.

tail, with a full complement of engineers, yard workers, and ticket agents. The line is only two kilometers long, but it has all the paraphernalia of stations, switches, and signals. It keeps up with railway technology in the PRC—as when the original steam operation was electrified ten years ago. It also has an enviable safety record—more than 35,000 kilometers without an accident. Its three hundred workers put in regular four-hour shifts several times a week. All are between the ages of ten and thirteen. Surely any thirteen-year-old would like to be the one in charge of the locomotive!

Yet in spite of all the talk about "usefulness" and "relevance" in Chinese education, these students do not graduate to work on the regular railroad. They, too, are sent away at fourteen to areas in which the local committees have decided that they would make good oilfield workers or pig farmers.

One of my uncles tried to explain the system to me.

He says that decisions about whether Young Chen is destined for fields of oil or of corn would never be left to Chen himself—or to his parents. Graduates are always directed into "suitable" and "useful" work through group discussion, committee meetings, and party policy (as in deciding that a particular area is to be developed). Although a student might display a talent or express an interest—in mathematics, for instance—the ultimate decision always rests with a group, a committee.

It was nice to discover that on the job, and on the streets when the day's work is over, these workers are individuals and not all-alike machines. Their personalities

Students at work die-casting machine parts in a middle-school factory.

were as varied as the girls' colored and brightly printed blouses. Even work overalls couldn't conceal the differences, as I found in talking to two of the machinists in Canton. Both had strong Cantonese accents and had spent their entire lives within Kwangtung Province—never more than twenty-five kilometers from their present factory.

Yet one of them, Fang, was what I would call a straight party man. It didn't matter what we talked about, he always sounded as though he had been prerecorded in Peking. Perhaps he had memorized his lines for the benefit of visiting China Tour groups. Whether he talked about work or play, his words could have come straight from the pages of such PRC journals as *China Reconstructs*.

Next to him worked Yip, five pounds lighter and one year younger, but otherwise he looked like Fang's twin. Yip, though, was quite outspoken. When he referred to standard speech, he used the familiar term "mandarin." When I asked him about some vegetable stalls along a Canton street—expecting the stock answer about "sideline occupations" and the small plots of land allocated to commune members for "personal" use—I couldn't believe his answer (in English):— "They are making extra money with a black-market shop."

Such differences of attitude are even more surprising when you consider how close the Chinese work community is. Unlike American workers, who drive home when the day is done and may live fifty miles from their city job, the Chinese generally eat, live, and play as one work-related unit.

All the workers in one factory or school or hospital may live in one communal block of flats or a small neighborhood as tightly knit as if it had walls built around it still. Sometimes, the workers' apartments even have a curfew, with outer gates locked promptly at 11 P.M. And the factory or shop itself is the center for all kinds of activities. Instead of being a place to serve clocked-in time, as it generally is in Western countries, the Chinese work place provides everything from food and medical attention to education and entertainment. My cousins take all this for granted. I would feel stifled by the twenty-four-hour restraints of the Chinese work community.

The lack of school electives seems bad enough for anyone who has grown up in America. I cannot even imagine how it would feel to have no say about a career. Yet I did not hear any of my cousins or their friends complaining about the lack of choice. Their contentment is only partly the result of growing up where majority needs and group discussions are taken for granted. Their system has some advantages.

The Chinese do not get an oversupply in some professions—like the unemployed teachers I know who have to switch to jobs such as taxi driving or door-to-door selling, in which their professional training is irrelevant. Many of them may think their college preparation has been wasted. But no one in China would feel that way—all jobs are of equal value.

Perhaps we should adopt the Chinese attitude toward all kinds of work. The son of the neighborhood doctor in Canton does not seem at all worried that he is probably going to be the first member of his family *not* entering the medical profession. He says, "It makes no difference what I do. Every job is a good job!" For in China today, there is no distinction between "head" work and "hand" work.

In the past, villagers held intellectuals—and landowners—in great awe. Everywhere, scholars received special respect, and intellectuals came to think of themselves as "better" than field-working villagers. An intellectual would not even carry a package. ("It is beneath my dignity.") A rural, uneducated dialect was cause for disdain and mockery. The speech of the man of learning—the mandarin class—became the national ideal.

Today, you are not supposed to use the old term *mandarin* for common speech because of its association with this discredited class, whose false pride is by no means an invention of modern Communist propaganda. Sixteenth-century accounts written by Europeans speak of Chinese people "worse treated by these mandarins than by the devil in hell," and they contrasted the ordinary "plain" people ("humble and obliging") with the mandarins, who "set themselves up as gods." The old mandarins, who served in one of nine grades of government service, are gone. But my experience suggests that their modern successors can be found in the petty officials of the thirty grades of modern government service. To a Western visitor, at least, the tyranny of the mandarin seems to have been replaced by the tyranny of the committee.

But no worker is thought to be superior just because his work involves more "head" than "hands." There is just as much merit in working as a hotel maid cleaning the toilets as there is in being the top man or woman responsible for running a twenty-seven-story building. Everyone is "a serviceman for the people." Receptionist, dining-room supervisor, head cook, floor washer—all are to be addressed as "Comrade" (*tung chih*). The same term is used in addressing a worker in the fields as well as someone who has been given advanced professional training. It is difficult for visiting Americans to remember that these comrade-workers in hotels are morally outraged if they are offered tips.

It is difficult for me to understand a world in which there is no concept of a "better" job—the reason I was sent to college and friends moved to other cities. It is hard for some Chinese-Americans who have been brought up to

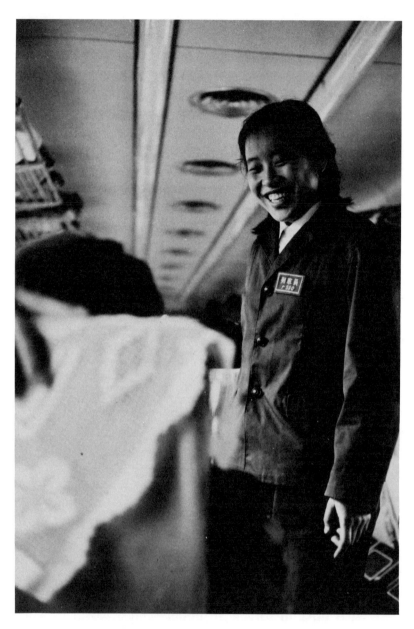

A traveling worker. On the train carrying foreign visitors from the border to Canton, this girl provides tea, beer, box lunches, and some English conversation.

save their money, buy property, and go into business for themselves, to find when they arrive in China that their relatives see nothing admirable in their success. Instead, the relatives see only failure—moving "down" to the discredited roles of "capitalist" or "landowner."

It is one thing to be told about these attitudes toward work. But for the family visitor alone, observing the Chinese on the job is not as easy as it is for visiting groups of tourists. After all, an American bank teller arriving at work with an out-of-town relative who wanted to sit behind the counter and "observe" would soon be in trouble. And I doubt that the union would let my dad take along a visiting Chinese uncle "just to see what goes on." Even the most public-relations-conscious American company, eager to hand out promotional literature and to provide tours through the plant, prefers to keep its visitors in company-structured tour groups.

Members of "friendship groups" sometimes participate in a kind of exchange program with their Chinese counterparts, but I did not qualify. Nor did I like the idea of factory work as spectator sport—the kind of Travel Service tours my uncle continually tried to get me to join. Their carefully structured interviews and briefings struck me as tiresome. I wondered if the workplaces on those itineraries had been dressed up to serve as showcases for Chinese achievement, and I thought that I would have a better chance of observing real behind-the-scenes workers on my own. My experiences were limited—and would have been impossible without the help of Uncle Chen's party-committee friends. But at least I spent some hours watching and talking to workers, and making my own small discoveries.

My first discovery was a new meaning for that familiar word "factory." The small electronics factory was not an enterprise that had been taken over from discredited foreign (or local) "capitalist exploiters of the masses." It was a highly efficient operation that had been started originally by a group of housewives. There are factories like this all over China. They began in the 1950's, when there were shortages of parts and equipment in every field. Women were not yet fully integrated into the general work force, but they were filled with patriotic enthusiasm and determined to help their husbands build a new China.

And so they began their support industries. No visitor to China can escape the story of Taching—where housewives salvaged scraps of work clothes and improvised linings for padded jackets out of ragged fur caps, eventually developing a highly efficient tailoring operation. Other housewives at Taching salvaged scraps of metal; they ultimately started a factory to forge new tools. Neighborhood enterprises in other areas began with such primitive jobs as hand-hammering ball bearings and then went on to redesign a drill press or furnace for greater efficiency. Some women came to their task unable to read even fifty ideographs, yet they ferreted out theoretical and technical information, designed, constructed, and tested. Before long, they were not only reading ideographs but also complicated blueprints that enabled them to place and solder a thousand components on a single piece of equipment. One housewife-founded electronics factory even provided parts for China's first earth satellite, and others developed precision parts for computers.

It seemed as though all the workers I met would rather tell me about these accomplishments than talk about their own jobs. With traditional Chinese humility, each one would say, "Oh, my job is very ordinary"—even though to me the individual pride and the meticulous workmanship looked quite different from the assembly lines my father knows. But I should not have been surprised, after seeing the well-made products turned out by the children at Chen's school.

Another surprise was that being sent to the country did not mean—as I had supposed—that the assignment would necessarily involve working in the fields. Factories in China are not confined to what we think of as manufacturing areas. They are scattered about the countryside as part of a program of rural industrialization. Instead of having a rural population drain, as we do in the United States when country children leave for the cities, seeking a wider range of opportunities in technology and trade, the Chinese children can go to work in modern industry while they still live down on the farm. The general direction of young workers is not away from the land—as it is in most parts of the world—but back to it, as each year new groups of middle-school graduates from city schools are assigned to regions needing more hands.

When I finally got to a commune myself, I found that the rural industries generally emphasize local needs. They do not have to consider profits or export quotas, as we do in the West, so they can concentrate on irrigation and drainage equipment, farm tools, or fishing boats. At the same time, a country boy or girl (native product or city transferee) might just as easily be working at a rural iron-and-steel works or helping to manufacture the latest laser spectrometer. One of the political meetings I attended had for its subject the development of another feature. They had just set up a typical "extended production line." At one end was their new twenty-horsepower tractor plant. Feeding into it were a whole string of smaller rural factories, one making diesel engines, another fabricating parts, a third concentrating on crankshafts, and so on.

At the textiles factory, I was introduced to one fellow with a thick country accent. In the canteen, we got to talking about this business of *where* workers go. He explained that he had been transferred to Canton just recently, from a commune about two hundred kilometers away. His previous work had been on the brigade seed farm, but the committee selected him as one of a group who would work for nine weeks in Canton—training for setting up a spinning mill back home.

Trying to find out precisely why he had been chosen was much more difficult. As in the schools, where my suggestion of "special" needs or abilities always seemed to shock the teachers, Sheng-li and the other workers denied that transfers or promotions are ever related to "special" aptitudes. In one of his cynical moments, however, my young Hong Kong uncle suggested that the best qualification for advancement in China is membership on the party committee. (Needless to say, Uncle Chen—who has served on a party committee for years—vigorously denies such favoritism.)

Certainly no one in China can do as workers employed by big American corporations can—request a transfer. Sometimes real hardships are involved—and the cousins cited several cases of desperate workers who tried to arrange an exchange through a factory bulletin board or even an announcement in the street (tacked up at a bus stop, in one instance). Most of the workers I talked to, however, seemed to think that such exchanges are very selfish—even when the worker has been separated from a sick parent or from spouse and children.

I began to think that no one in China has any say in either the kind of job or its location, and it seemed as though what we think of as talents would never be recognized, although Eileen told me that "barefoot doctors" are usually selected from workers who seem to have a particular aptitude. Cousin Wang had a better example, although it may just have been one of his modern fairy tales.

According to his story, there was a girl working in a Canton hotel, a hotel jampacked with foreigners attending the trade fair. Her cleaning chores did not give her much direct contact with the foreigners, and her grade-school English scarcely qualified her to talk to them. Nevertheless, the few contacts she did make were remarkably successful. She had a way of soothing "difficult" Western guests. After three years, the local party committee must have decided that her talent was too good to waste. They sent her off to the Foreign Language School in Peking, and she is now a very successful interpreter.

Her job is one that most American students might covet—traveling, meeting new people. But I would hate most of the assignments that will be waiting for my cousin's friends. None of the jobs sound interesting. They stand a good chance of being directed into the textile industry, which is of major importance in Canton and throughout China. Four hours among the clacking, whirring, grinding, thumping looms and spindles were quite enough for me.

Yet when the lunch break came and I sat talking with the workers in their look-alike overalls, there were no complaints. Neither were there any intimacies of shared hopes or talk of their outside lives—although I later found out that their lives are not quite as drab as I had supposed. Detecting my negative response to their working conditions, they all seemed to be quite determined to show me that they are really part of one of China's modern marvels.

And so for a side dish with my salad I got the usual pile of statistics: more than 14 million spindles and .3 million weaving machines, manufacturing more than 10 billion yards of cotton goods every year—three times the Japanese output, 3 billion yards more than the production capacity of the United States or the Soviet Union; in Canton

Kwangtung province's traditional arts include famous ceramic wares, such as the delicately carved open-work vases of Fengsi.

China's Foreign Trade

alone, one plant with 3,000 automatic looms was making more than 1.3 billion yards of cloth. . . .

Canton is best known for its textiles and such enterprises as cement and fertilizer plants, flour mills, sugar refineries, food processing, leather goods, bicycles, scientific equipment. It is also noted for embroidery. I have seen many elderly Cantonese women doing this work in San Francisco. Young Chen had spoken so often of any job being "good" that I thought I had a fine opportunity to tease him: "Maybe they will send you to the embroidery shop, Young Chen!" I was happy to see that he and his friends briefly dropped their earnest discussion of work assignments and produced one very small giggle.

Apparently, the local residents still concede that

A group of girls work on some of the lace fabrics produced in Soochow and other areas.

China's Foreign Trade

women have a "special skill" for embroidery—and they even have some quotations from PRC leaders to prove it. There is another exception to the open-to-all work assignments—craft skills that were traditionally passed on from fathers to sons and grandsons. When I was able to talk to a

carver of ivory (another Cantonese specialty) and a lac-
querware artisan, I found that, like the cloisonné workers
in Peking, all had a family connection—sometimes twenty
or more generations long. Such artisans and others with
"inherited" skills, however, make up only a very tiny segment of the Chinese work force.

Whatever the job, "equal pay" is the rule in China. To
me, though, it sounded more like equal poverty. Historical
perspective helps. My mother tells about one employer who
"paid" her grandfather a bucket of water and half a cup of
poor-quality grain. Yet even today the average income is
considerably under 100 yuan (about $50.00) a month,
with a two-worker household averaging in the 150-yuan
range. One lathe worker I talked to earns 50 yuan, a cotton
cleaner earns 70 yuan, beginning teachers and doctors,
between 56 and 60 yuan.

There are eight grades for workers, beginning at 36 to
40 yuan in most low-skill assignments, but still rarely paying more than 75 yuan for someone who has additional
duties as committee chairman. Chen and his friends may
get even less than 36 yuan for their first two years as
trainees, although they will be provided with lunch and
work clothes. Eileen has an aunt who teaches in middle
school and has reached the grade of experienced worker,
earning 90 yuan—a little more than a clinic's staff physi-
cian. Maximum for Eileen's aunt will be about 140 yuan, 5
yuan more than the average dentist, while top experienced
physicians and surgeons can advance to 250 or so—the
same as the head of a factory employing six or seven thousand workers. Eileen heard of a senior ("first grade") professor in Peking who was receiving 345 yuan. In 1979, the
government plans to raise all wages.

I was told that the uncle who has party duties and the
equivalent of Western-type managerial responsibility will

A commune worker pats mortar between the adobe bricks of yet another new building.

eventually get a higher-than-average salary. If he reaches the heady upper limits of party leadership, he could get even more than 255 yuan. But it is quite impossible to get precise figures on these modern mandarins.

But I was surprised to discover how small the outgo is from the average worker's low salary. Auntie says that only about 5 percent of the family income goes to rent and utilities—although that varies, depending on whether the family lives in a centrally heated apartment block, and on the size of the family. But the rent of between 3 and 10 yuan per month is related to the size of an apartment alone, so that two rooms in an ugly block would be no cheaper than two rooms around my family's pleasant courtyard.

When I asked some of my lunch-table friends what they spent their salaries on, they seemed puzzled—as though that, too, were an area without choice. There is no income tax. Commuting costs are virtually nonexistent—partly because of the system of providing low-cost housing near the job (and dormitories for unmarried workers and for workers transferred away from their original base). Bicycle purchases, they said, are authorized on the basis of need. Most of them had received the necessary permission, although one or two were still walking or taking the bus while they waited for their names to move to the top of the list.

What about health costs? I asked—a real problem for most Americans, even when they have substantial union benefits. My granny paid about five cents for a visit to the local clinic in Canton. Most medical services are at least partially prepaid through contributions at work, with various additional small charges for medicine and hospital services. In a country where the wages are so uniform, it is easy to identify anyone who cannot pay for treatment and who then receives free treatment. One of Granny's friends had even been sent to Tsunghua Hot Spring, about eighty kilometers from Canton, so she could bathe in the 45-degree Celsius waters. This was not a pleasure trip but an attempt to cure her stubborn arthritis, which had yielded neither to something called "sea-snake potion," nor to the usually effective acupuncture.

Working conditions seem to be good—at least in comparison with some of my parents' memories and the descriptions of labor conditions in the 1920's, or even compared to the fields and factories of twenty-five years ago. The eight-hour day, six days a week, seems to be average, with a brief lunch break that often has to be used for sports practice and "impromptu" discussion (some of these pep talks sounded more like the political-education classes to me).

Every worker drinks on the job, but the beverage is tea. As in the homes I visited, there always seemed to be a thermos jug ready, with lidded teacups right on a workbench or desk. No one seemed to "waste" time on a tea break. When I asked about it, the lathe operators pointed out with the patience of keepers dealing with a lunatic that leaving their work "just to drink tea" would result in spectacular drops in production figures. This doesn't sound much like the people's attitude in England, where workers went on strike when their (generous) tea breaks were shortened. And I cannot imagine the workers at Dad's plant forgoing coffee breaks.

My lunch breaks with the workers were also quite unlike my experiences in American cafeterias. At the textile plant, the electronics factory, and a paper mill, the lunchrooms looked more like jail facilities: bare tables, enamel mugs, tin bowls. Workers supplied their own utensils, including chopsticks. Food was very plain, with little choice —salad, soup, noodles—although I heard that some factories have "ethnic" cafeterias, catering to workers who do not eat pork. Most of the workers had no experience at other factories, but the three or four who had been transferred said that they remembered more wheat products at a plant outside Peking, and lots of bean curd as well as sizzling spicy dishes in Szechuan shops. I was disappointed that no one seemed to have eaten such "exotic" items as a Mongol dish of cheese with sour cream, butter, and sugar, and a serving of mutton-on-the-bone.

We had to bus our own dishes—and wash them too! I almost missed seeing the handy food catcher, a nice economical touch that one of the girls at the paper mill pointed out to me. There was a little grid under the faucet, to catch any scraps for the local pigs. But after all those clean streets, it was a bit of a shock to see that bones and gristle often got dumped on the table during meals and that several workers emptied the dregs from their teacups right on the factory floor.

Many of the cafeterias are also open for family dinners and for breakfast. My uncle and aunt regularly eat a low-cost meal at work just before the 6 A.M. workday begins. They also find the factory canteen is useful for getting together with Young Chen—either at Uncle's factory or Aunt's workshop—when evening meetings or classes make it impossible for them to gather at home. Unfortunately, they were not encouraged to use cafeterias as places of entertainment for foreign cousins, so that is one experience I could only enjoy occasionally.

Times when workers actually stay on the assembly line after regular shifts are rare. The Chinese have a principle of "combined work and rest" that discourages overtime—except in cases of specific emergency or some urgent local or national production goal. As the son of a union member in good standing, I was surprised to find that such overtime work is not paid for at time and a half, with extra at weekends.

I kept asking, "Do you have much overtime?" But the response was always a blank "Overtime? Oh, we do not do that!" The answer was the same when no party worker was present. Later, one lathe operator said that he does not even claim "straight" time when they stay on for special jobs. Claiming extra pay for extra hours would be "selfish," especially if the period was short. Even more strange—one night when I went to a meeting with Auntie, we passed the door of a workshop and I could see five or six workers still at the bench. She explained that there had been a power failure earlier: these men and women had come back, on their own time, "to finish the job."

Another surprise was in the attitudes toward moving up the ladder of responsibilities in the egalitarian Chinese atmosphere. There is no concept of "executive suite" or "key to the executive washroom." Instead, they have a precise schedule to determine how much time the upper echelons will continue to labor. A coal-mine leader must return to the pits for one hundred days a year, a commune's brigade leaders must spend a minimum of sixty days quarrying stone for animal pens or tunneling through a mountain. For someone at Uncle's rather low level of party responsibility, committee duties and work-place leadership must be taken care of in his "spare" time!

It seemed like a lot of drudgery, with too few incentives for me. Yet like pioneers in the American West, the workers I met were all zealously breaking new ground and scornful of hardships on their new frontiers.

I had not thought of ports or shipyards as "frontiers" until I met neighbor Fong's son, who was home on a weekend visit. He described Chankiang—a former French concession—as a frontier in terms of jobs, and said that the work at Chiangnan Shipyard could be regarded as an industrial frontier, building ships for an expanded merchant marine. Young Fong said that the new ports and facilities (like those Eileen saw in Shanghai) would rival any in the world.

When the last United States ships sailed out of Shanghai in 1951 with their cargo of silver dollars, all China's port workers were men. Tugboat captains, pilots, and technical personnel were also invariably foreigners—as they had been in all the Treaty ports since the mid-nineteenth century. Now, the workers are all Chinese, and right beside the men you can see women operating cranes or helping to run the computerized port operation. Another aspect of the waterfront scene was also very different from the picture my father had described—the terrible poverty and scrawny opium-addicted laborers have vanished.

When I got home to California, some of my friends were surprised that the Chinese are now building their own ships. But after all, the Chinese devised the first watertight compartments—a vital feature of modern supertankers and cargoliners. They also had the earliest mariner's compass—a "south-pointing instrument"—about 200 B.C. Perhaps my doubting friends should have been reading *China Reconstructs* instead of Western textbooks claiming that China has only one auto plant and "little in the way of industry."

Actually, there are thousands of factories making everything from ball bearings to engines and tires, with a quarter of a million workers in the auto industry alone. There is an entire new city (Changchun) where the first auto plant was built in 1953, and they now also make trucks, rolling stock, and such products as chemicals and textiles. China in fact has a dizzying range of export goods.

The silks and spices that lured the first Europeans to Cathay over the old Silk Road through Mongolia are still being exported. But the modern export list goes far beyond an exotic catalog printed in Macao in 1590: leaves, "loaves," and "twine" of gold; camphor, cinnamon, musk; and the porcelain that is now an expensive antique for European and American homes. Even my ethnic-studies courses had not told me of some of China's contributions, such treasures as ginger, copper, iron, silver, lead. One important export was rhubarb, commonplace in the West today, but a wonder cure-all when Europeans first received it from China.

China is not entirely self-sufficient. She imports raw materials, grain, some machinery. But the country is obviously not a land of backward peasants grubbing away at barren soil and lacking natural resources. Tucked away underground, there are more than 1,500 billion tons of coal, 25 billion tons of iron ore, unknown reserves of oil. China's resources run all the way from A (alum) to Z (zinc). In between you could list aluminum, antimony (the world's biggest deposits), asbestos, chromium, copper, gold, manganese (third biggest), mercury, molybdenite (again, the world's largest deposits), nickel, phosphorus, potassium, silver, tin, tungsten, uranium, and more—including enough salt in the Charhan Salt Marsh to last for eight thousand years.

Now, after twenty-five years of embargo, we in the United States are once again importing carpets and cotton goods, tin and raw silk, and—just as in the days of the great China clippers—we are eager to drink Chinese tea.

I disliked the continual cataloging of modern Chinese wonders—especially since the catalogs were often accompanied by actual or implied criticism of Western achievements. Sometimes the lunch-table crowd sounded like students in a rival school, bragging about the superiority of *their* team. And I still have serious doubts about the apparent virtue of all those volunteer propagandists. Surely a whole nation has not been converted into paragons of public-spirited virtue, all striving only for the good of the PRC instead of for such earlier rewards as jade bracelets and gold teeth!

If I were a worker in Canton—where overseas Chinese and foreign visitors are especially visible—I doubt that I would be so docile or so enthusiastic about being sent away from my city home to labor in the sheep pens of Inner Mongolia. What is the secret of the Chinese worker's apparent contentment?

7

TWO-WAY MIRROR

IT WAS DIFFICULT to understand the apparent contentment of the Chinese people, but by the end of my weeks in Canton one thing at least was clear: The good or bad aspects of job assignments and recreation activities alike look very different from Uncle Wang's or Elder Cousin Chen's point of view than from mine.

I usually saw the lack of freedom, the lockstep schedule, life without midnight snacks, pizza parlors, personal telephones, television programs, my own car. It all seemed unbelievably tedious. But my Chinese relations showed me that even the most exhausting hard labor had for them all sorts of hidden pleasures. I tended to pity them for the way in which they were limited to group recreation, their lack of any private leisure. They in turn showed me that their recreations are as suitable for their life in China today as the sailboats, skateboards, and motorbikes are for my friends at home.

Instead of complaining about the lack of choice in job assignments or bemoaning the six-day week or the extent to which even "free" hours are preprogrammed, my aunts and uncles continually reminded me how much better life is now than when they were children. Sometimes, it sounded as though they felt compelled to try to persuade their odd foreign nephew that they are indeed quite satisfied, thank you. I have to admit that they showed me some unexpected freedoms in their circumscribed lives. There are even areas in which ordinary, unskilled, poorly educated workers are treated with more dignity than their American counterparts.

The robot image I had formed from watching crowds moving daily from work to committee meetings to political-education classes certainly did not fit my off-duty relations. They could grumble and quarrel and laugh and cry just as much as I can. The main difference is that they have considerably less time in which to do so—and most of their energy is needed for an activity-filled life that all of them have actually been conditioned to *enjoy*.

They have also been encouraged to develop an unusual range of hidden talents—as the textbook authors whose work I had seen in cousin's classroom, as well as in their new roles as inventors, artists, musicians, and even as the teachers of "expert" scientists and doctors.

Cousin Wang rattled off hundreds of examples of worker-authored textbooks and of the worker ingenuity that I had heard about in neighborhood factories. For once, it was more interesting to listen to his earnest, statistics-filled lectures (sometimes sounding as though he had been programmed in Peking) than to tune him out! His tales included the enterprise of workers faced with shortages of metal. They had solved the problem by chiseling hunks of granite into machines for thread-cutting, boring, and drilling. Other workers had actually put together machines made entirely of wooden parts.

I later noticed a similar ability to improvise out in the fields, when one of our team members fell and broke her arm. Two of the team made a lightweight splint from nearby branches—willows, I think. Instead of ripping a shirt into strips for bandages (the extravagant method I learned in first-aid class), one of the boys gave her the shirt off his back. This was not the sacrifice you might suppose. He used the "barefoot doctor method" to fold the entire shirt, so that he could wear it again as soon as it had been washed. I also had a glimpse of the ingenuity of the barefoot doctors themselves when one, who had been working with another team, hastened over to help and began scraping a vile-looking substance off her belt!

It was certainly an efficient way to carry a first-aid kit, but I rather wished that I had *not* asked for the details of the poultice she applied—especially when our on-the-spot paramedic said that it also made an excellent pain killer, to be taken internally. She explained that the belt is made from braided daphne bark and clematis roots, following a recipe in her official manual. She wears the belt around her waist whenever she is out in the fields, and all that is necessary is a quick scrape for instant filling of prescriptions. The scrapings are usually dissolved in wine—but the accepted in-field substitute is "boy's urine." Moreover, she said: "The more the daphne-and-clematis belt is soaked with perspiration, the better it works. . . ."

In contrast to such primitive but effective do-it-your-self projects, the Chinese industrial scene is filled with worker inventions of quite unbelievable complexity. When I hear that workers at Changchun are responsible for 6,370 technical innovations (470 of them described as "major"),

Barefoot doctor cycles off to the clinic.

or that once-illiterate port workers have been responsible for one hundred innovations (including new methods of loading and unloading ore), I am skeptical. It seems incredible that half the designers of a new chromatograph mass spectrometer ("accurate to one part in a billion") were "experienced workers" with no advanced training in physics or mathematics. Having had some experience with American high-school committees that could never agree on anything, I simply cannot imagine committee-designed equipment.

Yet on the commune, I did see some of these products in use, including a portable lightweight projector that workers had designed and built for traveling film crews. Uncle

Chen said that the precision components of his watch resulted from "worker innovations" at the Shanghai factory.
And my new friends out in Kwangtung Province were continually pointing out items—including an infrared carbon-
dioxide analyzer for plant photosynthesis and a laser device
for treating seed—that they claimed had been designed and
built by workers whose formal education had not gone beyond the primary grades.

It seemed strange, too, that workers who have no
choice in what they do—or where they go to work—display
so much inventiveness in the role to which the various committees have assigned them. Doubly odd, to me, was that the
committees, who seem to pay no attention whatever to individual wishes concerning job assignment (and who con-

One of the many do-it-yourself vehicles on the streets
of China today.

tinually insist that "all jobs are good jobs") actually pursue a national policy that pays so much attention to the worker's *ideas*.

Just so long as the ideas are job-related, of course!

It is easy to feel superior as you listen to simple-minded slogans that include Five-Good Soldiers and Five-Shovel Brigades, and it is difficult to imagine American workers being inspired to new wonders of production by clouds of rhetoric, by Mao's essays, and by the twin cries: "In industry learn from Taching!" and "In agriculture learn from Tachai!" But I began to suspect that I was missing the point. Perhaps I could get more done, too, if I borrowed one of Mao's texts: "If conditions . . . seem unfavorable, create the necessary conditions and go ahead!"

When I was in China, however, the continual citing of Mao as inspiration tended to obscure the very real accomplishments. I even came to dread opportunities for unstructured conversation lest some eager young worker approached me with yet another tale to show how Mao had inspired his colleagues. A particular source of pride was always the worker's ability to put one over on Western experts—the word "expert" invariably having bad connotations in China, suggesting an inflated self-image.

The favorite example of inspired and innovative workers is Taching—a tale told so often in briefing sessions as well as in books, essays, and movies that I could have recited long passages from the soundtrack of *The Pioneers* from memory before my three months were up. The success at Taching originally sprang from a desire to prove that American engineers were wrong when they said that the oil could not be developed commercially, and then that Chinese workers could get along very nicely on their own, without the Russian experts who replaced the Americans.

There was a time when gasoline was so short in China

that Uncle Wu remembers Peking buses running on bags of methane (carried on their roofs). But defiant Taching pioneers took core samples, set up foundries, recycled tools, and developed a sophisticated water-injection process. Today, you see fields of grain planted right up to the small brick pumping stations, an automated operation tended by white-smocked men and women. The supposedly worthless field supplies crude oil, petrochemical fibers, and insecticides. Oil is even exported. And it all began with a handful of determined, mostly inexperienced workers, living in tents and dugouts and hauling supplies by muscle power and camel cart.

When I visited the factories, someone was forever at my elbow pointing out a piece of equipment that had been invented by "an old worker" or some local "middle peasant." Yet no one ever did explain satisfactorily how Mao's rhetoric (in the essays "On Contradiction" and "On Practice") could substitute for technical ability—as when a near-illiterate worker invented a photoelectric meter "to regulate combustion and eliminate smoke."

I think the real credit lies elsewhere—but in an equally strange way of working. At the electronics factory, Chin-hua had been soldering away at routine circuits for almost ten years before she had an idea for a better product. She lacked the technical training to produce the circuitry, so an engineer with more advanced professional qualifications was put to work as Chin-hua's "assistant"—a role-reversal that has not yet caught on in American factories.

To see her—once again back at the bench, soldering iron in hand—you would never have imagined that this woman in smock and white cap was one of those "experienced workers" always being credited with inventions. Yet such workers—many of whom have only a primary-school education—are often credited with "teaching" a professionally qualified engineer, pharmacist, or scientist concerned with the development of new products or machinery. Eileen even saw college-level textbooks authored by combined teams of workers and professionals, or by professors who had been sent out of their labs to undergo on-the-job training by sheepherders, rural herbalists, or coal miners before they compiled texts. Doctors of medicine are regularly sent out "to learn from the people." Even an advanced research institute sent its scientists out for practical field study. Engaged in lung-disease research, they were put to work in a coal mine, to see just what it feels like "to work and breathe dust."

Among the mountain of data thrust upon me by the eager Wang cousin, there were even more esoteric credits for worker-teachers. Members of the technical staff from Shanghai's Futan University were trying to duplicate a two-thousand-year-old bronze mirror. They consulted workers from a nonferrous metals foundry in the area, and "together developed new techniques for application in contemporary optics" (also duplicating the efforts of the ancient bronze masters, apparently). Similarly, Peking University—whose scholars scarcely even acknowledged the existence of "peasants" in the past—actually consulted "old farmers" when they began to study 7,000-year-old rice seeds discovered in Chekiang Province.

After years of demonstrating against the military establishment in the United States, I found it difficult to accept the national enthusiasm for yet another group of worker-teachers—the soldiers of the People's Liberation Army. This affection did not seem quite so strong in Canton as out in the country—at least none of my relatives seemed to be singing the praises of the military, and one of my aunts holds to the old-fashioned notion that all soldiers are louts.

Yet the workers in the factory cafeterias, like the commentators in movie and TV programs, seemed to talk about "admirable" soldiers almost as often as they were telling tall tales of worker accomplishment. I got rather tired of Good Little Boy Soldiers and the heroes of the Long March, and I had to keep reminding myself that my Chinese cousins are just as entitled to *their* heroes as American schoolchildren are to admire Washington, Lincoln, or Lee.

The admiration felt for PLA soldiers is one aspect of Chinese history that Young Chen could talk about. He has been raised on stories of the days just after the establishment of the republic in 1949. Often the only available workers then were soldiers. They helped local residents to get industries started, to set up administrative machinery, to replant crops. Eileen reported that they also became invaluable teachers in the field of public health—not only preventing postwar epidemics, but also helping to eradicate pests, and to establish new standards of hygiene. And in contrast to other countries, where soldiers are often blamed for spreading venereal diseases, in the PRC they are credited with the educational program that has eliminated such diseases from the modern Chinese scene.

All this earnest doing of good works and all the tales of inspired invention should not obscure the lighter side of the worker's life—even though the "combined work and rest" of PRC theory takes such large bites out of the "rest" segment for team sports practice, committee service, and a rugged program of after-work classes.

I thought it might be fun to sit in on some of the classes, a good opportunity to see my cousins' fellow workers in a more relaxed atmosphere. But what a mistake that was! About three fourths of all class time was allocated to political study (including those twin Mao essays). Current topics during my stay were "Denounce the Gang of Four" and various aspects of the latest Mao volume (posthumous publication of the fifth volume of Mao's essays and speeches), with a graded reading program depending on the worker's place in party politics (a two weeks' crash course for officials, six months' for the next level, and, for my production-team friends in the commune, just selected passages).

It was incredibly dull in such classes—the closest anyone came to argument or controversy was in picking on some hapless lathe operator who had not shown a "proper" grasp of an obscure point of ideology. I asked my uncle if anyone cut class. "Never!" he retorted, although I got a rather different impression from a commune meeting later. In Canton, everyone in class seemed unbelievably earnest and much more attentive than I would have been if someone forced me to study the workings of American government or to read the Nixon-tapes book five nights a week.

Most of the other classes were job-related, including some technical short courses that I would have found more useful than Mao's essays in developing new machines or circuitry. There were no degrees awarded for this course work. And I looked in vain for the kind of "enrichment" courses we have in community colleges and high schools at home. Adults in China cannot sign up for night classes in home decorating, French cookery, or sex techniques, although in the commune I did find some fun courses, with talented artists and high-spirited actors.

I had my first glimpse of worker-artists in Canton, at a most unlikely place: the factory bulletin board. It would have been easy to miss the examples among all the neat, businesslike announcements—most of which were too technical for me to read anyway. But those strips of colored paper with beautifully written ideographs . . . Surely the factory hands were not writing poetry?

Chieng-ming was pleased to translate and to explain

how much "better" these verses were than the poems on our scrolls at home. This especially elegant display was apparently designed to impress visiting tourists; usually, Chieng-ming said, the poems were just chalked up on a board ("we don't like to waste paper"). But it seemed strange to find that the aristocratic tradition of reading and writing poetry has now been taken over by factory hands and farm workers.

My father used to urge me to study calligraphy, and he liked to cite the old scholar-poets. He went to school at a time when many intellectuals still scorned fiction. (Back in 1722 it was even worse; one emperor ordered that the *Encyclopedia of Chinese Literature* should omit all such works.) When I complained about tough college exams, my dad reminded me that entrance exams for the Chinese civil service used to require that candidates compose poems on prescribed themes.

Some of the factory poems would have made the snobbish old scholars twirl in their graves. Today's poets prefer to describe "A Veteran Worker's Hands," or to "Sing of Anshan Steel." They write of bulldozers, dynamite blasts, and a bumper harvest, just as the bulletin board I saw had lines on "Our New Furnace" and "Worker Chan Comes Back from School." Later, I read some of Peking's translations of verses by a Mongolian Five-Good Soldier, a crane operator on the Shanghai docks, and Shanghai's very own collective, the Dockers Spare-Time Writers Group. Even writing poetry seems to be done by committee! And when the PRC National Anthem was revised in 1978, the words were "written collectively." One of my favorite verses told about virtuous Old Han—who, according to convention, should have been at his son's wedding, but as a good Chinese worker opted instead "to lead us in testing an automatic valve."

These poets—and the artists and amateur opera teams I met in the country—rarely seemed to step outside their political framework. It was disappointing for me to spend several hours "relaxing" with Young Uncle Fong or Cousin Wang, only to realize that their smiling public masks were also their private faces. I kept hoping that they would stop talking like Peking pamphlets and speak like "real" people. But to them, *I* was the strange one.

Walking home after class one night, with some young workers, I asked them: "How long do you have for your annual holiday?" But even that simple question involved a substantial communication gap.

At home, we go up to our mountain cabin during Dad's one-month vacation, and we get away for weekend skiing quite often. My sister just returned from a nine-day London theater tour with some other teachers. When one of our aunts could not get a visa for China, she used her two-week vacation from a San Diego menswear store to join a "fun" charter to Hong Kong.

My Chinese companions could understand my "family" reasons for coming to China—although whenever I spoke about wanting to study my Chinese "heritage," that seemed to baffle them. But they simply could not understand why my aunt would fly all the way to Asia just for personal pleasure. Instead of envying her opportunities for travel, they reacted with shock. One young worker—who will probably go far with his party superiors—said that in China "we do not practice such extravagant self-indulgence."

The expense and the length of holidays back in the United States seemed especially shocking to the twenty-to-thirty-year-old group with whom I spent so much time. Some of them lived in a dormitory and count themselves lucky if they can manage to visit out-of-town parents once a year, at the time of the three-day Lunar New Year break. Various transferees who were in Canton learning new skills had wives and children still continuing to live a hundred or more kilometers away (so that the wives could continue their essential jobs). One worker said that in three years of working in Canton he had not seen his wife more than once every two months. Among Cousin Wang's co-workers in the Travel Service, there are some who live in the dorm and can only get back to their families for at most one week a year. Yet all of them condemned as selfish the workers who tried to arrange private transfers through the kind of informal street notices I had heard about.

Theoretically, every worker gets about seven days of paid holidays each year, usually national holidays, with no additional vacation time. Some of my Canton family said they had occasionally had longer periods off—but always for such reasons as a changeover to new equipment at the plant, a shortage of raw materials, or a temporary assembly-line breakdown. A few of the modern national holidays coincide with the time of ancient festivals that are not supposed to be in favor now. Families used to visit temples during the mid-autumn festival. Now magazines show them putting flowers on a national soldier-heroes monument during the "new" autumn festival, October 1—the birthday celebration of the People's Republic of China. Instead of going moon viewing at the temple, they view memorials to "People's Heroes from the Opium Wars to the Present Time."

I just missed celebration of an international holiday —May Day, or Workers' Day—although Eileen had been in Peking for International Working Women's Day on March 8. She discovered a rather cute new custom: children presenting flowers to such new heroines as a woman tractor driver, a street sweeper, and a worker on (live) high-tension

Everyone loves a parade! Amid waving banners, red flags, and huge posters, girls wave long scarves and ribbons, their rhythm undisturbed by the boys' noisy firecrackers.

wires. Young Chen had a school holiday in May, the youth festival commemorating the May 4 Movement. All of these holidays include parades, firecrackers, and songs. But the only traces of the old celebrations I heard about were in connection with the New Year. (There are two New Year holidays in New China: one on January 1, and the bigger celebration coinciding with the ancient lunar calendar that was first observed during the Hsia Dynasty.) The Chinese New Year celebrated in February 1979 was the year 4677.

By American standards, the Chinese live a very spartan life, much too short on both leisure and cash. Even though I knew that China was not a consumer society like ours, I found it difficult to identify with families for whom one radio, one sewing machine, and one or two watches seemed to constitute the limit of ambition. Going without some of our creature comforts would not be too bad. I could give up my electric toothbrush and our automatic hot-dog cooker, for instance. But giving up my skis and my stereo, and especially my private moments would not be so easy.

Never having known this "decadent" life, my cousins seem untroubled by their group leisure. After the first few evenings, when I realized how peculiar my desire for "privacy" seemed, I listened to my cousins talking about sports and classes—and discovered that their life-long group conditioning had made them more comfortable in such groups, not at ease with strangers. No wonder that I always felt so isolated during my few solo lunches in Canton.

Personal motives are beyond the grasp of my cousins, and if Uncle remembers the old days when it was still all right to look out for yourself (because no one else would look after workers then!), his party membership seems to be very effective in keeping him silent on the subject.

How do you explain that you miss the pleasures of a Sunday sail on the bay to someone who does not even own a bicycle or a transistor radio? There was no way to compare notes with my cousins on the weekends I spent fitting twin mufflers or riding out to the beach in a friend's van. They have never even seen a car used for anything except official business. Always using equipment owned by school or factory, how can my cousins talk about a life in which surfboards and scuba gear are regarded as social necessities, as they are in southern California? I tried to imagine describing for my Canton family the favorite game of our San Francisco neighbors—a game played on the

Girl workers review the listings of new shows.

screen of their color TV. But the Canton family doesn't even know anyone with a small personal black-and-white set.

Yet the cousins and aunts and uncles all get along very well without our gadgets and games. I even began to suspect that once I left, the tape recorder my father had sent would be tucked away out of sight—an example of embarrassingly conspicuous Western consumerism.

They seem to have only about twenty-five really free evenings in the whole year, the rest of the time being so relentlessly scheduled that we didn't even enjoy many evenings out while I was in Canton. But I soon began to discover that my Chinese relations are as ingenious at finding moments of simple pleasure and relaxation as my ancestors were in inventing complex gadgets.

Many of the parks open at seven o'clock in the morning, so that the crowds on their way to work or school can enjoy the flowers and trees. At lunchtime, I saw some of the workers take their food to a nearby park, where you could always find rows of bikes lined up at the entrance. Muddy boots, oil-stained fingers, and factory work clothes showed that the seemingly carefree couples in rowboats and the leisurely strollers would soon be back on the job. On a rainy afternoon, I had expected to find the zoo deserted. Instead, I saw the usual crowds, many sheltering under umbrellas, but still enjoying the antics of the monkeys and the pandas.

Another favorite break in routine is a restaurant meal. To celebrate the return of a cousin who has been working out of town, my family usually goes to a restaurant in Liwan Park, where there are dozens of rooms connected by walkways over the water, and tree-shaded balconies from which diners can look out over the lake while they sit at enormous round tables. One night we enjoyed an exotic meal out that included a service comrade presenting a snake for Uncle Chen's inspection as casually as a waiter at home produces a live lobster. Occasionally when (rich) Uncle Wu from Peking visits, he treats the family to an expensive night out on Shamian Island, with such gourmet treats as jellyfish, sea slugs, and tender young dog.

But the tourists who return home obsessed by the "wealth" of Chinese food do not seem to realize that even the most senior workers (with those "high," over-100-yuan incomes) cannot go to the kind of place where tourists select from a thousand-item menu. The traveler eating a "cheap" banquet for about three dollars is eating up the equivalent of some family's monthly rent.

The most common family entertainment is a movie—with inexpensive tickets bought at work. I thought that the movies at least would provide an escape from political messages. What a mistake! Young Chen's friend, who was "criticized" in formal session for becoming a movie-addict, must have been a singularly obtuse lad.

Even the cartoons were political. The feature attraction my first night at the movies was the Chinese equivalent of travelog and costume drama—armchair travel to Tibetan pastures that most of the audience would never see. By the third movie night, I could have written the entire script myself, so predictable were the plots and dialogue—in spite of high technical quality in color and production.

Always there is a villain—someone operating on "bad political principles." Favorite villain figures are Chiang Kai-shek and his Kuomintang troops, landlords, and Western imperialist-capitalists. Heroes and heroines are seen with Mao on the Long March or leading workers against "evil" bosses. Sometimes there is a complete cast of hero figures, such as the builders of a dam or developers of an oilfield (always working in the face of great physical hardships and extreme ideological opposition). Action involves the triumph of (Communist) Good over Evil. The only suspense is the delayed re-education of minor characters, who usually follow the "incorrect" political line and have to be shown the True Way of Mao.

There are parallels to our war movies (their superb accuracy probably due to the fact that they are made by the Army's own August First Film Studio). Many of the epics of the Long March reminded me of old Hollywood movies about the Foreign Legion or some frontier outpost. But always there is the relentless political message, and the insistence that this drama is *true*.

It was quite a revelation to go to one of these shows

Peking opera, contemporary style: *On the Docks,* performed throughout China in the 1970's by the Peking and Shanghai Opera Companies.

with Young Chen and five of his school friends. I saw the deadly movies from quite a different point of view, while they identified with the boy-hero (a real-life figure, a genuine Chinese spy). Other dramas also include such "real-life" characters—these are not made-for-the-kiddies Disneyland adventures. And the girls have their own martyrs too, such as Liu Hu-lan, beheaded at the age of fourteen by Kuomintang villains. Everyone gets a share in hero identification, including the middle-aged mothers. In one movie I saw how the mother gallantly barricaded herself against a wicked landlord, tossed grenades and bricks upon the enemy, and even turned into a female Samson—pushing the burning walls of her home down upon her attackers.

You do not hear any criticism of "movie violence" in China. After all, the violence is all authentic. But in spite of the combination of genuine action and high adventure I always felt cheated. The "real-life" heroes such as Five-Shovel Brigade and Iron Man are disturbingly reminiscent of something by the Brothers Grimm. When the Iron Girls of Taching labored to fill a huge water jacket with tiny, tiny buckets, my memory flashed back to the tale of the witch and the princess, in which the poor girl had to labor over a pond, her one tool a hole-filled thimble.

In 1979, now that Chiang Ching and her crowd no longer control literature and entertainment, there is a wider choice of movies, including filmed versions of traditional Peking operas, as well as science fiction and comedies imported from Western countries. I cannot help wondering why anyone would bother to censor the dull films I saw, but then again, I was looking at them with my Western eye, instead of remembering that for my Chinese cousins these might be as exciting as a Hollywood epic on Lincoln and the end of slavery, or Washington defeating the British, or those spy films in which the villains are invariably either Russian or Chinese.

When the rest of the family was occupied with committee meetings, classes, and sports practice, Granny Chen sometimes took me along to watch the neighborhood TV. That, too, was relentlessly educational-political, with "news" often being interpreted as a visit by "sympathetic" workers and political figures from abroad, local rallies, national meetings inspired by Chairman Hua. I missed seeing the scenes of filmed weeping that showed precisely how members of this or that factory or Autonomous Region mourned first Premier Chou and then Chairman Mao. But I did see talk shows featuring local factory workers discussing the "errors" of the Gang of Four, and some travelog-type feature films much like those I had seen at the movie show.

Only the sports programs were really good. There are no blackouts designed to keep the local arena's attendance up. Since there are no private sports teams and no private companies trying to sell tennis balls or sets of skis, there is no "star sponsorship" of products. In fact, there are no athletic stars at all. Instead of our million-dollar contracts for football stars, they have a system in which all players are worker-athletes, with emphasis on *worker*. Team members may get extra time for sports practice just before a major tournament. But even after overseas tours (such as the

Two sides of China: private relationships and simple pleasures (couple hand-in-hand, left), while an enormous poster (right) inspires the workers with yet another picture of Chairman Hua, and more thoughts of Mao.

women's Asian basketball championship and the men's volleyball tour of the United States), it's right back to the workbench as soon as the athletes return to China.

Some China travelers say how much they enjoyed TV without commercials and highways without billboards. Perhaps these tourists did not realize that the "lovely" banners they described carried virulent political messages in their "flowing calligraphy." All the TV programs can be read as commercials for good clean PRC living. And I saw quite a few before-and-after ads too—instead of men and women transformed by the addition of a wig or the loss of twenty-five pounds, they show before-and-after scenes in a PRC coal mine. Instead of posters with seductive maidens and handsome men promoting toothpaste or cereals, the Chinese have those great posters of Mao or Hua urging increased oil production or the need for agricultural reform.

I missed reading the daily papers in China, too. Foreigners are not even supposed to read them (papers published by commune, neighborhood, and factory are classified as "private conversation," and I was not allowed to bring any copies away with me). Once or twice Granny Chen shared tidbits from her daily farm-journal-type items, a politically correct "Quotation for the Day," and a few human touches in the form of court reports showing that the Chinese *do* sometimes commit petty crimes after all. The uncles read a paper distributed through the post office, and I was really sorry that my knowledge of ideographs was not up to reading its letters to the editor.

The Fong uncle read out a letter to the editor that suggested its writer was actually *unhappy* with a work assignment. But old Uncle Wang and the pious Wang cousin immediately jumped in to assure me that they had never seen such a letter before. Uncle Fong laughed then, and said: "I just made that up for Young Joe. He is always looking for dissatisfied customers." My cranky uncle did not appreciate the joke. . . .

The only really nonpolitical evening entertainments apart from my brief escapes to the zoo were the occasional fireworks displays. The Chinese invented explosive devices centuries ago (about A.D. 200—and they even had a splendid stink bomb about 1150). Apparently they preferred to use explosives for fireworks rather than bombs, though, and this puzzled earlier Western visitors.

It is strange to think that one Roman Catholic missionary watched a display just like the ones I saw. He described the brilliant cascades of light, exploding bursts of multicolored flowers of fire, and firefalls lighting the night sky about the time that his fellow countrymen were exploring the New World. How odd that he regarded the Chinese as "backward" because they used their powder to make fireworks for entertainment. He thought that they could have fought "a great war for many years" with the "wasted" powder.

But perhaps my ideas about Chinese leisure activities seem just as strange to my Canton family. . . .

8

COMMUNE LIVING

CHINA'S greatest lure for me was the commune—the rural life of my father's childhood. What I really wanted to do was to settle down in a commune for a year or two, get the feel of China, work the land that so many of my family had left forty years earlier. Even Uncle in Peking and relations on party committees had not been able to arrange it by the time that I boarded the plane for Hong Kong, but I was confident that details could be worked out after I got to Canton.

I was wrong. There was no way for me to live on a commune for a year—or even for a whole month—in spite of the various "foreign friends of China" who have received permission. Now that I am safely home in California, though, it seems as if I had a very lucky escape. . . .

Before I left home, I thought that I knew all about Chinese communes. The color photos and TV news clips all pictured the life: white Peking ducks marching off to the dinner table; wrinkled old grannies holding the hands of toddlers wearing brightly colored pinafores; workers smiling and singing as they planted rice or chiseled out rocks for a new hydroelectric project dam.

I expected to meet girls down on the farm too, like the one pictured with a tank of insecticide on her back, her hands close to those of "a young agricultural worker." Perhaps Communist life had not been entirely desexed, after all!

In Canton, Cousin Wang introduced me to two friends —Lin-yip and Po-lam—who were off for summer work in a provincial commune. When they managed to get permission for me to go with them for two weeks, their lectures about what I should do and say as their guest, for whom they would be responsible, seemed a small price to pay for the privilege.

By the time we got to the end of the hour's journey from Canton, we seemed to be pretty good friends. Both knew enough English to help out when my Cantonese was not quite up to the speed of local conversation. It was a pity that they sometimes sounded like the *Little Red Book*. But they were both party members in good standing, and I could always tune them out and enjoy the view from the train window.

The scenes of farmhouses and fields, once we were beyond the suburbs of Canton, could have been a replay of scenes along the track from Hong Kong. It was easy to let my mind wander. . . .

But I should have paid more attention to Po-lam's briefing on communes, Chinese style—for nothing I had heard en route prepared me for the shock of the first twenty-four hours as a very inexperienced production team member.

At home in California, communes are filled with free spirits who have dropped out of a materialistic society.

One woman tending geese might seem to be no different from rural Chinese workers of a century ago, but she is part of a modern commune with a population of 63,200, which has its own factories, clinics, and hospital, as well as schools, film team, and three hydroelectric power plants.

They sometimes have a special interest. One commune I know is a nudist colony, another a clan of self-confessed anarchists. Most are like one where my friends live on the Mendocino coast.

They built their own cabins, did their own plumbing, have a share in a local midwife-nurse co-op. Days they spend more time making pots and doing embroidery than milking goats or growing corn. They eat a lot of organic stuff and brown rice, and take a dim view of the neighbors, whose major crop is marijuana.

In the evenings, we sit around and talk. Small kids wander in and out. It is impossible to figure out which mothers and children belong together. I play my guitar, someone else has a flute, and there is mellow music out on the porch while the sun goes down. The oldest person I have ever seen in the house was my thirty-five-year-old aunt, who had come along to help set up a batik-dyeing project.

We arrived at the commune. Instead of finding myself with an extended family practicing learn-as-you-go farming, I was in the midst of something resembling California's gigantic agribusinesses. Instead of two dozen easygoing friends living in homemade redwood houses, here were fifty thousand strangers living in carbon-copy concrete —houses of better quality than those provided for migrant workers in California's Central Valley, but uglier. The general layout was less like rustic Mendocino than like southern California's look-alike bungalows—but reduced to half scale and with the California swimming pools exchanged for pigpens out back.

The first person on the scene had nothing in common with the smiling greeters of TV films. He was a frowning, leathery old man. And he did not come out with extended hands or proffering the inevitable cup of tea. He came out mad.

There was no way that the tour guide in the park could have persuaded foreigners that this angry voice was really just using the tones of normal Chinese speech. Even if you did not know a word of Cantonese, *his* tone was unmistakable. And once again I thought of the tyranny of these officious new-style mandarins.

The welcoming speech was a bureaucrat's tirade, reproaching us for late arrival. "Was there no earlier train?" Surely we knew that work is supposed to begin at daylight. "See how many work hours we have neglected!"

My sponsors seemed humiliated to be found guilty of such "selfish" behavior (although my foreign weakness for oversleeping was to blame). To me, the lecture sounded more like a school principal's stern reprimand to naughty children than a way to communicate with adult workers. On the other hand, it was quite a relief to see this human crack in the smiling face of China.

Bureaucrats the world over seem to have a knack for making life hell. This one, for instance, didn't believe in wasting a second. We had five minutes to go to the dormitory with our things and change into proper work clothes. That wasn't too hard. All we had to do was unroll our sleeping quilts—the "suitcases" most workers use when they are transferred. Fifteen minutes later, we were out in the fields, and we really were getting our feet wet.

Much of that first day remains a blur. We had missed the morning breakfast break, the sun was hot, and everywhere around us were men older than my grandfather and children younger than my smallest cousin. All of them were casually hefting irrigation pipe, hoeing and digging, running blithely about carrying baskets filled with stones —baskets that I couldn't yet lift five inches off the ground.

All I could do was concentrate on the tiny square of dirt at the end of my hoe, and all I could feel was the sweat dripping off my nose.

Any idea that the pace of Chinese living might slacken out in the country was quickly lost. By the end of the second day, I was already putting in the standard twelve hours of hard labor—not all of it in the fields. Since I came home, I have looked again at some of those glowing descriptions of commune life written by Westerners, and I wonder what they really saw.

Perhaps they visited only in their imagination. Or their "work experience" was carefully programmed by PRC hosts to create such favorable impressions. I only know that most of their descriptions are closer to life in a holiday resort or a YMCA summer camp than to anything I saw in China.

There was not a single day that I did not feel too tired to appreciate the "beauty" of sunsets color-washing the harsh buildings of concrete and brick. There wasn't an hour that my back did not ache, or my hands and feet were not blistered, cut, or chapped. And instead of relaxing in a hot tub to soothe my aches, I had to make do with a pan filled with cold water in a bleak concrete bathhouse—not at all like the elegant Chinese baths, hot and cold, that had impressed Marco Polo at a time when Europeans went all winter without even changing their clothes. The few bathtubs there were uncomfortable, small concrete tanks. Usually we just showered in an open-fronted stall.

After a day of finding out that it is easier to chop down plants than to hoe between them, you do not have much energy for questions or discussion. There is no way to describe just how weary you feel at the end of the day. Or the depression of washing up, eating a quick supper, and then having to drag out to one of the eternal meetings.

Workers with baskets and hoes reflect China's continuing use of people-power. About 97 percent of the workers in this area are still involved in agriculture.

I would have preferred to stretch out on my bunk with a book, but the light was dim and the only permissible excuse for staying away from the perpetual organized activities was sickness. How I longed for my tape deck, the sound of music. . . . Unfortunately, "music night" was not until Thursday and turned out to be a heavy mix of PRC inspirational songs and scenes of dam building and corn sowing masquerading as dances. Only once did I hear a tune that my mother used to sing, but the old folk melody was now used in praise of increased steel production.

Not that the dorm itself would have been an inviting place in which to linger—it would have made a county jail seem like a health spa by comparison. Beneath its dim light fixture (a fluorescent lamp aptly referred to as a "flicker light" in England) were the double-tiered bunks usually occupied by students attending rural branch school or city workers undergoing "re-education." A wooden table, three straight chairs for eight of us, open shelves for our clothes. No decoration apart from a rather tattered poster advertising the last traveling exhibition of "Art by the Peasants of Kwangtung Province."

That word "peasant" required some explanation—and my two political coaches were eager to correct my assumption that the term had become obsolete during Europe's Middle Ages or been discarded with the end of various colonial administrations. In the People's Republic of China, "peasant" is both a technical term and a label that identifies one of the country's modern-day heroes.

People's communes developed out of the cooperatives that had been organized when the Communist government first came to power. At the time of the 1949 Land Reform, villagers were classified as "rich," "middle," or "poor" peasants. The rich hired others, the middle group only farmed their own lands, and poor peasants always worked for someone else—either rich peasants or the landlord class. One landlord and two or three of the rich peasants might own 75 percent of the village land, while the rest of the villagers had only tiny plots. In 1949, the land and personal possessions of landlords and rich (or "upper") peasants were distributed among those without land—but this led to a good deal of bickering over divisions of land and property, from those who received as well as from those who were obliged to "give."

Then one group of fifty-six "advanced co-ops" (thirty-eight villages) organized themselves as the Chiliying People's Commune. Mao liked the name—derived from the Paris Commune of 1871—and established a nationwide program on August 29, 1958, which gradually organized all of China outside the major cities under this scheme.

The extent of this organization is frightening to anyone accustomed to lazy weekends of sun and surf or even to someone who has grown up on a working farm in America. The lack of privacy I had felt so acutely in Canton was here intensified—every minute programmed with work and "revolutionary" study or team-oriented sports activity.

You cannot even go to the toilet alone. Many of the old-style individual privies were said to breed flies and spread disease. Now, each group of dorms or houses has a pair of five-hole rooms (one each for men and women), strictly for squatting, and without even a partition between the holes-in-the-ground. Perhaps I was unduly sensitive: the local residents apparently receive early conditioning, judging by the rows of children on potties I saw when I walked past the commune's nursery.

All day long, from the first moments with communal bathhouses and toilets, I found myself caught up with the crowd—finally swept along to the nightly sessions, as I was even at the end of my first day's work.

One night it is politics, another pig breeding, the third night revolutionary literature or group poetry-writing class. My first meeting even featured a visiting petty official from the local (Communist) party committee, come to see that rumored idlers were no longer causing a drop in the usually spectacular production figures.

My two solemn escorts from Canton made sure that none of the nuances escaped me—although I noticed that they were rather vague in their interpretations of a discussion about a vanished twenty-five-year-old (had he run off to Canton or even Hong Kong, perhaps?), and in the reports on several workers who had apparently been reporting sick too often.

I was beginning to enjoy the thought that some of the commune's workers might have human weaknesses after all. But I did not stay smug for long. There was a short welcome speech for "our comrades from Canton." This included a rambling anecdote by the team leader about the last group of elementary schoolchildren and their follies—how they had plowed crooked furrows, chopped down plants, flooded seedlings. My companions from Canton carefully interpreted the technical terms and made quite sure that I did not miss the point—I was getting my first taste of those public-criticism sessions that I had previously dismissed as strictly the invention of hostile foreign observers, and I was Joe, the "bad" child.

The second day in the country was a real contrast to my second day in Canton, when I could stroll out and take in the city scene at my own pace after the rest of the household had left for work. Now I had to pull my aching body out of bed before daylight and join the march out to the fields, with only a cup of hot water ("white tea") for early breakfast. That was not quite as bad as it seemed. The real breakfast, bowls of rice porridge, was brought out to the field by a pair of arthritic grandfathers an hour or so later. They also delivered our lunch—a peeled yam.

In some ways, the work is not really so different from farm work anywhere—in spite of the PRC pamphlets that make it sound as though China's rural workers were continually engaged in heroic struggles to rebuild the landscape or tunnel through mountains (usually while undergoing plagues of biblical magnitude—hailstones, high winds, heavy rains, drought, insect pests, all within a single season).

But the whole environment is vastly different from our Western world of electric toothbrushes and dual-control electric blankets. I had been made aware of some of those differences in the first twenty-four hours with my family in Canton. That first-night banquet had been prepared with the same basic tools my mother uses: wok, knife, and long chopsticks. The food had been fragrant with the same traditional spices; there were jars of anise, cinnamon, cloves, fennel, ginger, pepper. . . . But there the resemblance ended. Instead of a double stainless-steel sink with dishwasher and garbage disposal, my city aunts had a cement sink and cold-water tap. No cabinets, no toaster oven, no waffle iron, no blender, and certainly no microwave oven. . . .

The absence of the appliances that we in the United States take so much for granted is the least of the burdens imposed by commune life. I was always worn out before the midday break, although there is not so much pressure as you get picking lettuce or tomatoes for hourly wages in California. It was just grinding, steady work—hard and hot. In some ways, the southern heat proved an advantage. Working through the noon hours in the south would give workers heat stroke, so we got a longer break than many people in the northern fields. And as our work took us farther and farther away from the dorm, we did not waste energy making the long hike back. Instead we relaxed briefly under a tree or against a retaining wall at the edge of the work area.

The national obsession against remaining idle seemed to operate even here. The men in China smoke a lot—Western campaigns against smoking do not seem to operate in this land of nationalized tobacco industry. Many would light up old-style pipes or a cigarette. There was usually some chat while we were actually eating—though none of the "happy singing" those imaginative travel-writers always seem to hear. More often, too, the chat seemed to center on questions related to work.

We were supposed to be taking a rest from the midday heat, yet I noticed that many of our group spent the time doing exercises or tossing a ball about. After a while, I too began to practice *t'ai chi*. It seemed to help my aching muscles a little. It also helped me to make friends.

One motherly woman confided that she had been terribly sick—"Only *t'ai chi* exercises helped me to do useful work again." She was always concerned for my welfare after that—offering little hints about the way to hold a hoe or lift a pair of baskets from the ground (at first, I thought that baskets dangling from a pole would either bounce right over the nearest precipice or deliver a karate-chop to my neck).

It was disappointing that I never did feel close to any of my fellow workers. The two most friendly members of the team—two about my own age, whose talk suggested they had grown up in Canton—always seemed to be separated from me by a protective wall of the other workers. My friends from Canton always seemed to steer me away from these two and from several older men who may have been former landlords being properly "re-educated" through labor on the land. But as so often during my weeks in China, direct questions—when I dared to ask them—were often ignored as "inappropriate" and answered only with discreet silence.

One afternoon I got a glimpse of something I had heard but not believed—the turning of work into a team sports event. Thinning rows of plants turned into a kind of relay race, with much cheering of five-person groups and victory shouts by those who got ahead of the average score.

I could not imagine field workers at home showing similar enthusiasm for the labor of picking artichokes or cotton. Yet in China I even heard of a commune where a team made a "high-speed mountain-climbing contest" out of their task of reforesting a 900-foot mountain slope. Even before my eyes were open in the morning, I could hear these sports maniacs practicing for upcoming meets of basketball or swimming teams, though I had no wish to go splashing off in the ice-cold stream. It seemed that no one was exempt: grandpas and the ten-year-olds pulled together in the tug-of-war; kindergarten babies waved scarves and leaped through hoops; and grannies who ought to have been doing embroidery quietly in the shade were out in the sun sharpening up their *wu shu* routines.

The hectic pace of activities slackens a little on Sunday, although just as on farms in other countries, there is always some work that must be done. Again and again I tried to figure out why everyone kept so busy—were they afraid to sit idle, even when they had no chores?

It may be that the pace at other communes was slower, that my impressions were colored by my own exhaustion or disappointment. The cousins in Canton were surprised that I had such a hard time; they regarded the commune experience as a break from middle-school routine and a chance to get away from their families and lark about a bit. Perhaps I was simply unlucky, my timing was wrong, and I arrived just as the group had been caught up in a campaign to "improve efficiency." According to Uncle Wu, the farther you go from Peking, the closer the residents come to skipping political-education classes and other inspirational events. . . .

At least I am glad that I could discover for myself just what a commune actually is. Most visitors think they have "visited a commune." But what they have seen is only a single production team, the basic work-unit. There may be three hundred of these teams in one commune. My team was typical—fifty households, with about 210 people (not all of working age).

In my corner of Kwangtung Province there were fifteen teams making up a single brigade—the unit that is

Mother and baby pause in the doorway of their home, en route to the commune's nursery. Note bamboo pole for drying clothes at left; also mother's print blouse and baby's gay assortment of prints and stripes.

responsible for day-to-day organization of larger overall activities. Our ten brigades together formed one commune.

Sizes throughout China vary. A commune of 25,000 to 60,000 members is common, although the range extends all the way from about one thousand to a huge group of 80,000 or so. Typically, a commune of 50,000 members (9,000 households) is an efficient agribusiness that does much more than farm about 100,000 *mu* of land. Under one great bureaucratic umbrella, they run clinics and hospitals, fertilizer plants and irrigation projects, schools and technical colleges, and many of the shops and services we would expect to find in urban centers.

Instead of finding one man working at a single loom, as in Mendocino County, in China you see a 2,000-spindle spinning mill. And in spite of the seemingly primitive toilet facilities, there is usually a very efficient wastes-management system that is linked to the basic economy of the pig.

The frugal Chinese tradition—that old joke about using every part of the pig except his squeal—has elevated the pig to a symbol of modern Chinese prosperity: "One Pig for Every Person; One Pig for Every *Mu* of Land." A pig rooting around the floor of a rural house in a TV film is not a stage prop, but a weakling being carefully bottle-fed in the family living quarters (where houses still often have dirt floors). Each pig is supposed to provide three tons of manure a year. Added to otherwise useless scraps, human wastes, and small quantities of chemical fertilizer, the pig manure provides compost to nourish one whole *mu* of cropland.

Thus even the most insignificant parts of the commune are fitted into the pattern of a whole nation—providing a startling contrast to the Western communes that are so often founded as a means of escaping national affairs. The commune even has its own militia unit, part of the country's national defense system. And at the top bureaucratic level there is a party revolutionary committee responsible for overall management, operating a sophisticated trade network, overseeing schools, and coordinating every aspect of local work with national goals.

The efficient operation at every level always impressed me. After my experiences in California, where communes and home carpentry were always closely associated, it was a surprise to find that Chinese communes have well-run brick and tile works, a shop to forge and repair much of the farm machinery, tractors for the use of the smaller units (production teams). There was even a brigade-run department store, though not quite up to Canton standards, and a team-operated supply center that was a cross between a corner grocery in an American city and a rural feed store.

Our brigade, like many others, corresponded to an earlier village. And that accounts for some differences in size. For instance, Sungchuang Brigade has only thirty-one households (190 people)—smaller than the average production team. Other brigades I had heard about had their own pig-breeding farms (selling weanlings to members at three fourths of the state price), flour mills, a phosphate fertilizer plant. Sometimes a group corresponds closely to earlier clan organization, as of the Chen or the Yang family. Occasionally a commune—for example, the 53,000-member Fengyi People's Commune in Tali Pai Autonomous Prefecture—is made up of six different national (ethnic) groups.

After I got back to Canton, I was able to use some of my time to find out more about the range of communes, their infinite variety, and the few exceptions to the usual pattern. Occasionally, a traditional crop (such as Dragon Well tea) gives the tightly knit group an excuse for keeping out strangers and the usual city-transfer newcomers. Yet even when an area once had a regional specialty—such as cotton or sugarcane or tobacco in the south—the modern trend is toward self-sufficiency and diversified crops. One fishing community on the coast can serve as an example. They have developed a secondary industry of panning for industrial garnets on local beaches, using this "sideline" in turn to pay for new fishing boats; they have developed an offshore crop of kelp; and, following the success of their rope and fishnet factories, they are talking about adding a boatyard and even a lab for the production of iodine.

Such ingenuity is impressive, but it is difficult to appreciate the accomplishments in human terms. Fortunately, my father's native village was not too far from the spartan dormitory—part of a related brigade, member of the same commune. Before I returned to Canton, I made the forty-minute walk over the hill, for another—and too brief—experience of a warm family welcome, and an understanding of some of the aspects of rural living today that I could never have obtained under the watchful eyes of Lin-yip and Po-lam.

9

MY FATHER'S COUNTRY

I HAD BEGUN to fear that the China I wanted to see existed only in my father's imagination. The Canton family, for all the warmth of their welcome, probably found my way of talking and thinking as foreign as I found theirs. In the commune dormitory, I remained a stranger among the modern residents of my father's native country. No one I met seemed interested in talking about the past or about our shared cultural heritage. Everyone was relentlessly looking forward, apparently trying to wipe out four thousand years or so of history.

Only when I finally arrived in my father's native village did I feel that I had come home to the land of his memories. This at least looked like the China I had imagined—the land where country people have maintained traditions, in spite of past tyrannies of mandarins and landlords, hardships of flood and famine, and centuries of devastation by warlords, Japanese, and Kuomintang troops. Perhaps there are other such villages hidden beyond the tourist pathways, and perhaps they too look much as they did a thousand years before Columbus sailed for America. . . .

My first glimpse of the village was a pleasant contrast to the harsh outlines of my production-team dormitory. There were only a few of the modern, look-alike houses, all at the outer edges of a community of dark-red brick houses just like the ones my father had described. Old trees softened the landscape, typical South China flowers grew everywhere. Even the pigpens were out of sight behind the walls. And right in the foreground, as though posed for my camera, were several chattering old grannies, with a group of five small children at play.

The power lines overhead and the new pumping station seemed to disappear as two splendid old gentlemen and a boy about my own age came toward me from the shade of an old, curved archway. "Welcome," said my cousin in his middle-school English. *"Huan-ying"* (Welcome) and *"Ni hao"* (How are you?) chorused the elders. Here at last was my country family—and here was the house where my father had listened to the fireside stories told by his grandfather, and watched his mother and grandmother as they raised their precious silkworms.

We walked into the postage-stamp courtyard, and just as my father remembered, there were three rooms, each no larger than our kitchen at home. But the family group was even larger than the one of his childhood. Now the household included five adults, seven children, two ducks, and a pig. The ducks lived beneath a tree that would be bright with persimmons in the fall, sharing their puddle-sized pool with great-uncle's three carp (who came plopping to the surface to signal feeding time).

Introductions were simple: Great-granny and two aunties sharing one bedroom, widow aunt's two teenagers sharing a bedroom with three cousins, Uncle and Aunt and their two "babies" (aged three and seven) in the double-duty living and bedroom. One of my welcoming committee lived next door—the old schoolmaster, now close to ninety. He remembered my father, took pride in the old scholarly tradition, and was quite unabashed in his use of the term "mandarin" for standard Chinese speech, and in wearing the long, formal robe that clearly identified him as a survivor of the old intellectual class.

The welcome was cautious, as it has always been in rural China for anyone coming from "outside," even one with my authentic clan ties stretching back through fifty generations of village life. As in Canton, we began with a banquet, here in the simple country style of cabbage soup, pork dishes, home-grown fruit, and a plate of duck eggs. Our ability to talk was limited by our accents. Apparently I sounded even more strange out here in rural Kwangtung than I had on my arrival in Canton, and their speech sounded just as strange to my unaccustomed ears. I was grateful for the school English of my cousin, but occasionally I had to resort to sign language.

We did not have to filter our private conversations through party-trained interpreters, however, as most travelers must. Gradually our conversation shifted from my news of the family in Canton to news of the California connection. As we talked, I realized that China's modern travel restrictions—when workers need a pass to travel beyond their immediate area—have made California and Canton almost equally remote for the villagers. Yet in my father's day any ambitious boy might make his way to Canton, to Hong Kong, and finally to America—although many families had to subsist on short rations of bran and millet then, and others had to beg.

Work today seems to be a safe conversation topic throughout China—a neutral area, in which day-to-day assignments can be talked about, while avoiding "trouble-some" personal and political subjects. Running out of family news, I therefore talked about life as a member of a production team. Great-granny was very concerned about the absence of some nice maternal figure to watch out for my health, even when I told her of the sympathetic *t'ai chi* practitioner. She was pleased to hear that I had been given a local remedy one night when my cough kept my dorm-mates awake—a mixture of chrysanthemum flowers, lico-rice, mint, mulberry leaves, bulrush, and an obscure plant that most botanists have never heard of. I had also been offered a preparation of ground-up wild date pits in case I still could not sleep, but she took a poor view of that.

Granny was very worried about my safety in the fields. She said that I was lucky the old snail-borne disease had been wiped out—the disease celebrated in Mao's poem "Farewell to the God of Plague!" But what did I carry along for snakebite?

That was when I got an introduction to rural medicine that went far beyond the cough medicine and the simple remedy my mother used in California—sliced ginger and green onion for chest colds. And no one had ever told me the contents of the hundreds of mysterious little drawers in the San Francisco herbalist's shop. Granny was eager to share her knowledge, and had one of the children write out directions for her antivenom prescription.

When I learned her "secret," I decided that I might prefer the poison to the cure. Said old Great-granny: "First take some cucumber slices. Then you must soak them in urine for about a week. You dry it one week more. After that you can wrap it up and carry it along to the fields." When she finally understood that I would no longer be working in the fields in two weeks' time, she suggested something "not quite so good," but very easy to prepare.

I doubt that it would be any easier to take: "tobacco-pouch washings"—the prescribed dose being two-bowlfuls——"swallowed as fast as possible."

Such traditional medicines are one aspect of the past that Mao was very enthusiastic about—having had plenty of experience of folk cures and readily available herbal medicine during his years as warrior-fugitive. Country people have a vast store of such remedies today, and the new-style "barefoot" doctors can identify and prepare local herbs—sometimes crushing as many as twenty different plants (out of a total of close to five thousand) for a single prescription. They also use Western pharmaceuticals, and their manuals list both—with the traditional medicine first.

Great-granny also talked about ginseng—good for everyone over sixteen, except during summer hot spells, she said, although most of its advocates in California are older men (who think it gives them more energy and endurance). Some of the Western travelers who heard about ginseng during China tours acted as though they had made a new discovery. But Marco Polo had already described it seven hundred years ago. A variety of ginseng grows in Canada and the eastern United States, of course, and in the 1830's this was exported in American ships to break the earlier ginseng monopoly of the Chinese emperor. The root of the plant looks much like a man (in Chinese, it is *jen-shen: jen* = man)—a fact that may account for some of its supposed virtues and those of the similarly shaped European mandrake root. There is more than superstitious value in ginseng, however. Modern scientific analyses have shown that the root contains calcium, iron, potassium, and vitamins, as well as rare earths and glycosides. My father says American ginseng is not one hundredth as potent as that growing wild in China's Kirin Province.

Like my old aunties in California, the country granny

worried that my flushed face (the result of my long, hot walk, I thought) was a symptom of some *yang* illness. She was referring to the theory that underlies all Chinese traditional medicine: the guiding principles of *yin* and *yang* (harmony of light/dark, male/female, wet/dry in Chinese cosmography). Everything in the universe is supposed to have *yin* and *yang* aspects (not simply the "male and female" principles identified by some translators—there is a very complex system relating *yin* and *yang* to physiology).

That afternoon, I watched other villagers come with bowls for their share of a communal home brew, a little something that the local medics had whipped up to combat an intestinal bug that had been troubling the workers. On weekdays in my unit we had a similar lineup, for cups of "heat-stroke medicine," and Auntie said that the small children in the family attended a regular public dispensing of "spring immunization," to protect them against measles.

I am glad that my Westernized mother did not give me the brew that is served to some of the Kwangtung children for mumps—the honeysuckle blossoms and forsythia sound quite romantic, but what about "mummied" silkworms (cocoons) and crushed, toasted "snake moltings"? It would have been interesting to collect some of these recipes—the barefoot doctors' manual is filled with such ancient cures—but most of the homely hints struck my Western ears as strange.

Yet it was good to enjoy the unfamiliar feeling that people really cared about my welfare. As I had already realized in Canton—in spite of the seeming coldness toward strangers—once the Chinese people get to know you, they are still among the kindest and most gentle on earth.

Of course I found out soon enough that village life was far from idyllic even here. The loudspeakers continued to nag with messages of political uplift—although the family assured me that it was not necessary to play the raucous wake-up exercise music that was played in my production-team area for the benefit of slug-abed city trans-ferees. The residents of this lovely old community also had their share of ideological hangups—including the ostra-cizing of a former landlord, now demoted to one of the smallest houses on the outskirts of the village. Yet there were other ex-landlords and formerly rich peasants who seemed to be living in their old homes (although without their earlier quota of servants and concubines). And, like the elderly schoolmaster, they were apparently accepted—and even respected—by the most rabid party-committee members.

I realized, too, that the various people who seemed to be just sitting about when I arrived had, in fact, given up their usual activities in order to wait for me—a standard courtesy for a guest. Ordinarily on a Sunday they would all have been out and about in group doings, just as in my commune over the hill. Even out here in the country, idle-ness seems to be an unknown concept. As I looked around, I could see villagers busy with the essential Sunday chores —tending their private vegetable plots, pruning backyard fruit trees, feeding pigs or ducks, getting together for the usual sports or classes.

Like Canton, this is a world without Sunday excur-sions—no lazy days at the beach or slowly swimming in the river (any swimming is practice for a forthcoming competition or "important military training"). A few dedi-cated sportsmen and women were preparing for a competi-tion by going off on a nice long-distance run in spite of the sweltering South China weather. I could see their blue and white shirts flashing along the distant paths.

Sunday relaxation does not include any of the all-day bike excursions that some tourists have claimed to see. I found even fewer personal bikes in the countryside than in Canton—and always for work, not play. Contrary to returning journalists, there is not "a bicycle in every country parlor," any more than there is a watch on every country (or city) wrist, or a radio and sewing machine in almost every home. According to my statistical coaches Po-lam and Lin-yip, there is a rural "average" of one bike for every two families and a sewing machine in only one household out of four.

I did glimpse some moments of relaxation from my dorm windows, too, when families sat outdoors on warm summer evenings. Sometimes I saw a group of old men there playing chess or card games. But the scene was never as peaceful as Portsmouth Square at home, and I did not see any of the old-fashioned canary fanciers comparing birdsong, as they did in my father's day. Still, such moments were a step closer to the Old China I had hoped to see than anything I found in modern Canton.

During the rare unstructured evening hours, children scrambled about playing finger games or a kind of hopscotch, or they tossed balls and little beanbags back and forth. The aunties said that children still like the old games with cut paper, too, and they always cluster around the grannies for advice in cutting out New Year decorations.

Warm summer evenings also gave me a chance to eavesdrop, and it was quite a relief to discover that earnest Little Red Guards (renamed Young Pioneers in 1978), neighborhood-committee mamas, and proper party-committee uncles could occasionally be human and squabble, too. The commune families argued not only about crops and divisions of work, but also about who should be chosen as leaders, which members ought to be picked for the three university places, and whether the youngest Chan son needed a spot of group criticism before he pummeled yet another neighbor boy.

Only once did I hear a really serious complaint—and that may have been no more than the disgruntled expression of a doting mother (a type also known in the United States). She was saying that her child had been slighted in nominations for a college-entrance interview. So-and-so's daughter seemed to be "going in by the back door"—a process that has supposedly been stopped. The angry mama did not care if the back-door girl's family *had* been on the Long March, that her grandfather was a People's Hero. Nor did she see any reason for still being so grateful to that family forty years after the event that she should willingly sacrifice her own daughter's chances.

During my long day in my father's village, I did not have to resort to eavesdropping. For a while I could enjoy the status of "distant cousin," as we made the rounds of Auntie Fong's neighbors. One talked about a grandfather who had emigrated to California; she showed me souvenirs sent by that long-ago railway worker, unusual "objects," since Chinese workers then as now usually preferred to send cash instead of the exotic items that Western travelers usually send home.

It was amusing to see a miner's pan used for panning gold. One great-aunt had wanted to know how anyone could cook vegetables in such a strange "wok." A corncob pipe had been judged inferior to Chinese smoking equipment. They liked scrimshaw but agreed that the whale ivory work did not come up to the standards of Canton's ivory carvers. Other items looked like Indian beadwork, and there was even one of those embroidered nineteenth-century samplers with a Christian motto.

As so often in China, sometimes I felt like an intruder, in spite of kind words and cups of tea. My mother had reminded me that other countries simply do not have the American habit of "dropping in" for refreshments and chat, and I was always conscious that I was disturbing the family's usual routine. But I was very grateful for the glimpses of families who sometimes matched (but often did not) the stereotypes of recent travelers' tales.

In the country, even family size was different from the Canton style. The five children of my distant aunt and uncle are not an uncommon number here. Many rural homes were as spartan as they are supposed to be, complete with packed-dirt floor, bare wooden beams, plastered-over walls, strictly utilitarian furnishings. Others seemed to be filled with objects of family sentiment, inherited treasures of jade trees and porcelain bowls that we would regard as heirloom quality. Unfortunately, the inhibitions of my Chinese upbringing and the need to avoid embarrassing my relations made it impossible for me to ask if these elegant objects had all belonged to beloved ancestors—or if they had been acquired during the redistribution of treasures taken away from landlords and rich peasants.

It was nice to get a break from the ever-present Mao and Hua posters, and to see a few scrolls like those at home. It was also pleasant to discover that some of the modern houses on the outskirts of the village had been put up by young couples seeking a place of their own. In spite of all you hear about nonexistent private ownership, the communes often allocate a small plot of land to young couples. Saving their money or occasionally borrowing from commune funds, they buy the materials and do the work as a "spare-time activity." To say that they do not "own" these homes is surely to split semantic hairs.

With my rural family, I was just as hesitant about probing for facts on incomes and expenses as I had been in Canton. Back in the dorm later, I was afraid to ask my

Out in the country, the farming families maintain the old tradition of having many children.

ever-ready companion Po-lam, lest that provoke yet another flood of figures. So I was pleased when a group of children came to my rescue during the second week of commune work—much as children had rescued me from stock PRC scenes that first Sunday in the park.

One evening after work, they invited me to tea at the schoolhouse, not without ulterior motives—their teacher saw it as an unprecedented chance for them to try out their English lessons with a native speaker. They willingly provided facts to add to my aunts' account of housekeeping, commune-style. I already knew that commune pay is based on "units of work," with men usually earning slightly more for unskilled labor.

Is this because men work better? The children chorused: "No, no, no!" Men and women get the same number of units for tractor driving (about fifteen or more), for instance, but for unskilled work the realistic country folk recognize that men—being larger and usually stronger —generally perform about ten points' worth, while most women rate only seven or eight. (It is also the custom to give women lighter assignments at some times, as Eileen discovered.)

After each harvest (there may be several crops during the year), crops are divided, with fixed proportions for state, commune, and individual. Cash income is based on sales, less costs. There is also a small agricultural tax paid on the production team's income—but it has no resemblance to past taxes (such as 50 percent of the harvest going to a landlord, or forty different taxes once paid to the Kuomintang). Today's tax may be paid with grain or with other crops. The central government buys a quota, and this in turn earns priorities for the team. Selling 10,000 *jin* of silkworm cocoons could bring priorities for purchasing chemical fertilizer to increase the yield of mulberry trees (and hence to produce yet more silkworms).

Actual cash varies. Here it averages about 300 yuan per worker for a whole year. But rents are even lower than in the city (2 or 3 yuan a month is average). Food costs may be only 5 or 6 yuan a month, because families have their own vegetable plots, pigs, and poultry, as well as shares of communal produce. Each householder gets a sufficient share of the major grain crop (where I was, in Kwangtung, it is rice) to store away and feed the family for at least half of each year, sometimes three or four times as much. To country people, a supply of rice is *real* wealth, especially when they have other signs of prosperity, including piles of warm quilts in areas where once many people couldn't even huddle under a tattered jacket—or so my young school hosts claimed, perhaps quoting from one of their inspiring texts.

One thing was clear, even among the few families who invited me into their homes—past generations of alternating feast and famine have taught the villagers to use their new wealth cautiously. There are no signs of anyone developing an extravagant life-style—although I have to admit that opportunities for extravagance also seem to be nonexistent.

Of course I would not expect families to whom I talked for only a few minutes to open up suddenly with frank discussions of PRC life. Yet it did seem strange to me that in all my days of rural living—and even in the accounts of rural life that I have read since I returned home—no one seems to have shared my appalling sense of isolation.

I realize that the Chinese do not have our Western problem of keeping the children down on the farm. Apart from those few misfits among the middle-school graduates who cannot adjust to country work, everyone seems very content both with the work and the rest segments of what I would find a very monotonous existence. The rural industries have added new dimensions to the scene, and busy schedules of sports and classes leave little time for fretting. Yet I felt as far from Canton as if I had been shipped to the moon.

In America, no matter how far you live from the city, you can keep in touch through your own phone, the family car, and cable television. Some Texas and California families even own a plane. But none of those things are privately owned in China—and the communal showings of movies and TV programs scarcely distracted me from my intense loneliness. Tips on pig breeding or well digging might be more relevant on a Kwangtung commune than in Canton, but a graphic film on manure management was still not my idea of good after-dinner entertainment.

In my father's day, there were no movie or television programs. He has often talked about the evenings of his childhood. The family lacked money for oil lamps, and they sat listening to Grandpa tell stories by firelight. I am not sure that the electricity provided by the recent hydro-electric project has been an unmixed blessing. Neither the preachy movie and television shows, nor the books provided by the modern Library That Comes to the Fields

Rural kitchen. A bamboo pole for the family wardrobe and baskets, a group of covered jars for food storage, a wok for cooking . . . Although surrounded by walls of the house, this area is open to the sky above.

could tempt me away from such favorites as *Strange Tale of Nine Deaths* (an account of a real-life murder in Canton back in 1725), and the old detective stories. No wonder that on special occasions the small children still prefer to cluster around one of the elderly grannies to be told about the Hare in the Moon, the Jade Empress, fox fairies, and ghost tales by moonlight.

Today's children can read, although they do not study the classics that my father loves. But many villagers were unable to read before the various literacy programs started in 1949. Soldiers were often illiterate, too. One of my uncles remembers using his primer as part of the government program to "teach a soldier to read." Some of the late readers also learned to write (although mastering the ideographs if you do not begin as a child is very difficult); a few of these late bloomers have joined the ranks of rural poets and part-time playwrights. The literacy rate is now 95 percent.

Alas, none of their modern tales compare with the stories once brought to illiterate adults and children alike by the village storyteller. Many of those yarns were set in a framework that helped to spread Confucian ethics, Taoist beliefs, and the ancient myths of Kitchen Gods and Heavenly Dragons to the most remote corners of China. Those stories were also filled with humor, imagination, and high adventure. Some were later written down by scholars— much as professors in the United States record oral history or Indian legends. And that is how I found myself on the evening before I left the commune cast in the role of long-ago storyteller.

My friends at the school were curious about the "old" stories that I said my father knew—and since I was able to do the telling in English (thanks to a translation of the old scholarly note-taking) even their apprehensive Communist teacher could scarcely prohibit the brief entertainment. . . .

I chose one of my favorite detective stories, *The Canary Murders*. Detective stories are a Chinese invention (long before Edgar Allan Poe!), but often the "detective" is a magistrate who must act as judge and jury and sometimes goes out detecting (in disguise) in order to establish the facts of the case. Like a modern private eye, the magistrate often has assistants, and there are snitches among the criminal's neighbors, willing to identify the hiding place of missing property (or even a missing head). But in most Chinese detective stories, everyone knows who the culprit is right from the beginning.

My story was about a "heavenly" bird, prized for its talents as fighter and songster (a kind of oriole), and the time was 1121. I remembered to put in all the "commercials" that are an essential part of such a story—little jingles recommending virtuous behavior. My modern audience found the ancient warnings funny. They roared with laughter when I frowned and said: "The mouth is the gateway of disaster. . . . Keep your mouth shut and your tongue well hidden!" But like long-ago villagers, when I asked one of the tale's stock questions—"Now wouldn't you think that . . . ?" or "How many lives do you think were lost?" —they all joined in the answering chorus.

They all enjoyed the violent scenes when murder is committed and concealed. Like Western children watching a favorite TV show, they were caught up by the suspense (the wrong man gets punished, an innocent man is sought while the guilty one remains concealed). They applauded when the criminals are caught and punished. And after I had given the equivalent of the sponsor's triumphant message—an advertisement for clean living, "Store up good deeds and you will meet with good!"—the children also applauded me. . . . I remembered that I must be polite and return their applause. And then we adjourned for more tea.

Could it be that these ancient tales of Virtue Triumphant really are linked to those pious modern storybooks after all? Mao used the old story form during the early days of the People's Republic of China—with tales to promote commune life-style and agricultural research instead of the old Confucian ethics.

Today, a public storyteller is a very rare treat—the *kwai ban* accompanied by rhythmic tapping of bamboo clappers. Ironically, the only time I heard one of these, it was part of a TV program.

Although I felt so isolated in the commune dormitory, the evenings were not always dull. I even enjoyed a filmed version of one of the Peking operas, caught up in the enthusiasm of my fellow workers. But I had hated Peking opera in Canton and had found the traditional versions in San Francisco even more boring.

The group putting on an authentic performance in California wore exaggerated makeup, costumes of garish colors, glittering satins. They represented bejeweled imperial princesses and concubines, assorted mythical figures, and long-dead mandarins. Actors stomped about the stage, making wild gestures, using stylized movements, and at particularly dramatic moments striking a pose. Some of my friends enjoyed the show, but my ears are not tuned to the singsong high-pitched melodies used for dialogue, and I am relieved that modern performances do not last as long as some of the earliest versions.

I was afraid that the rural performances would seem as long as the sixteenth-century *Peony Pavilion,* which consisted of song sets and flute accompaniment that lasted through fifty-five interminable scenes and took several days to perform. But the rural audience recognized some of the folk motifs (not all of the operas are in the "Peking" form; there are Hopei and other styles too).

And then I had the rare opportunity of watching one of the traveling groups that work in the fields by day and put on a show at night. It was strange to see the sturdy hoers of weeds and haulers of rocks and water transformed in the commune's "theater" (the courtyard of what had once been the major landlord's house).

Now they were singing and strutting in splendid style, stomping their feet, staring wildly at climactic moments, their traveling orchestra augmented by various commune musicians. As on other occasions, the girls in the audience seemed to clump together—just as I was firmly clumped among the single men—but afterward we all mingled quite freely, and had a lot of fun being coached in technique by the more experienced visitors (who had also begun in a simple commune opera class).

I had not been able to keep the plot of the performance straight—it was something to do with a PLA victory back in 1946. Some scenes were ploddingly realistic, political meetings just like the ones I attended. Others were imaginative, including a group of soldiers skiing down a mountain, choreographed into a spectacular dance number. The hero made splendid four-foot-high leaps to indicate his dash through a snowy forest, and seemed to jump more than six feet into the air when he denounced the bandit villain.

Watching the visitors coach the commune's would-be actors was better. The traveling team explained the techniques used for battles (always rendered in terms of dance), and demonstrated some marvelous somersaults to be used in creating an "underwater" illusion on stage. It reminded me of the pleasure of amateur dramatic groups at home.

Silhouetted against a wall decorated with framed calligraphy, a girl prepares for one of the popular folk dances depicting water maidens, bringing in the harvest, or other agricultural themes.

I had begun with a hostile response to the heavy propaganda of the themes—"Victory of the exploited class" or "Counterrevolutionary crimes." I had bemoaned the "perversion" of the traditions. Now I had to recognize the simple pleasure of the modern performers and audience alike in the substitution of leaping soldiers and workers for the mincing, squeaking concubines of the earlier form. The high quality of the singing, of the musical accompaniment, and even of a script that was being prepared as a group effort provided further evidence of the high artistic level of many cotton pickers and rock breakers—the commune artists Mao described with "hoe in one hand and brush in the other."

Before I arrived in the commune, I had been put off by such slogans, and the often-repeated comment in the classrooms at young Chen's school: "Art is a tool for uniting and educating." Looking at the work in a traveling exhibition, I discovered that in spite of the slogans I could enjoy woodcuts, sketches, painting, and even "group compositions" (sometimes accompanied by poems), although I would have said that art by committee could only have grotesque results.

It was a pleasant surprise to discover that even the prosaic-sounding "Cabbages" and "Cultivating Cotton" were rendered in lively, bold colors—clear reds and oranges, bright blues and greens—with a fine sense of design. Digging a well was transformed into concentric bands of color, workers in the fields appeared from a distance to be all-over patterns or dramatic diagonal lines. Among the paintings in traditional style I even found the Chinese equivalent of a Madonna and child—but this was a young commune worker, bottle-feeding a baby lamb.

These glimpses and the farewell-to-our-visitor party held on my last night provided some hints of the pleasures to be found in the lives of my village relatives. Unfortunately, I have been spoiled by Western values. For me, it would be a life of isolation and tedium.

10

UP FROM SLAVERY

HAVING GROWN up in a household with two older sisters and an assortment of visiting "aunties," I had my own ideas about the role of women in China long before I arrived on the Canton scene. Yet I was still not prepared for the enormous differences in motivation between modern Chinese women and their liberated counterparts in the West.

Even the most macho male chauvinist cannot escape the vocabulary of Western liberation—women seeking self-fulfillment, realizing their potential, gaining independence. China has no such concepts. There are no consciousness-raising sessions—other than political—for either women or men. The operative words for both sexes are "Proceed from the interests of the people and not from one's self-interest or the interests of a small group."

The tendency of young Chinese to clump together in groups, and according to sex, made it even more difficult for me to talk to the girls among my relatives than to talk to their brothers. Besides the universal Chinese taboos about politics and the difficulties of understanding anyone who grew up within the modern Chinese framework, there are still other barriers between men and women, and certain subjects are regarded as strictly women's talk. Eileen proved a valuable source of information about the sort of conversations from which I was always excluded.

Many of my Chinese friends in California are just as inclined as I am to strike up casual conversations, but Eileen was raised in a more conservative household. She is always scandalized by my public behavior: "Do you always try to pick up girls at the beach?" She will not discuss with me topics that any American teenager would take for granted. She even prefers to answer questions about Chinese views on love and marriage and sex through a series of written notes! Her attitudes are a useful reminder that many of the qualities Western observers regard as typical of the "prudery" of the Chinese Communists are, in fact, a national rather than an ideological trait.

I arrived in China with sufficient knowledge of history to avoid stereotypes, and with some understanding of contemporary women's achievements. I already knew that few Asian women—and certainly not the Chinese—had ever been quite the pliant, downtrodden slaves described by the pens of Western romantics. I had read about such early female achievers as the poet Li Ch'ing (A.D. 1081–1141), or the tightrope walkers of Tang times (A.D. 618–907) who were recognized as more skilled than the male acrobats. On the other hand, my father had quoted Confucius often enough for me to sympathize with women, who were —according to his view—naturally inferior. I had also heard my mother speak about the birth of her younger sisters—their arrival was treated as a disaster, a financial burden the family could ill afford, so that her parents were quite happy to have their elder daughter marry my father before her sixteenth birthday and emigrate to America.

It would be easy to assume that in comparison with the past, today's Chinese woman is completely liberated. After all, she has no physical limitations. A team of girl workers (all aged between seventeen and twenty-four) calmly hoist hundred-ton beams for bridges, while others handle oil-drilling rigs, operate pile drivers, and tunnel beneath the ground for coal and iron. A woman can do just about any job that a man can, and women are found in every occupation, from auto mechanics, cotton pickers, and dock workers through the entire alphabet to veterinarians, well diggers, and zoo attendants. One third of the workers at the Chinese Academy of Sciences are women. A middle-school graduate may be assigned to wield a pick and shovel or to go out and pick cotton. Eventually she may be put in charge of fifteen hundred highway workers or reach the highest councils of neighborhood, commune, or province—as did Wei Feng-ying ("a model industrial worker") and Wu Kuei-hsien.

In theory, there is no bias against women in the upper echelons of government, but the continuing emphasis on the value of experience leaves the women—who were late entries into public life—at rather a disadvantage, always a step or two behind the leaders of Hua's generation. At the lowest level of committee activity, women are supposed to be among the members elected to represent each production team at the brigade level and to take part in administration or to be nominated for additional education. The elected leadership is supposed to have nine members—two elders (over fifty-five), three around forty-five, and the rest about twenty-five. The leader also serves on the (Communist) party branch committees. Peking tells you that if the leader is over fifty-five, the deputy is usually one of the younger members. And Peking insists that women hold equal responsibility.

Everywhere I went, I tried to confirm the role of women in administration, and everywhere I failed to see them in the numbers Peking implies. At the very top—the party members around Chairman Hua—you see that the majority are well into middle or even *old* age, and the party leaders are all *men*. At the Fifth National People's Congress in March 1978 a woman (Chen Mu-hua) was named one of thirteen Vice-Premiers of the State Council. The twenty Vice-Chairmen of the Congress included three women: Soong Ching Ling, Tsai Chang, and Teng Ying-chao. Among the deputies were Chen Yu-niang (noted badminton player), Lin Hui-ching (table tennis), Kuo Feng-lien (Party branch secretary at Tachai), and Pandu (woman mountaineer).

Yet movies, magazines, and modern operas are filled with stirring accounts of women who were real-life heroines. The movies I saw included *Boulder Bay,* featuring the magnificent Granny Tseng, and *The Pioneers,* with its Iron Girls. Any discussion of movies or books always produced some tale of former housewives who overcame cultural handicaps and performed Herculean labors at Tachai, reclaiming so many hundreds of *mu* of land all over China. They have their own girl martyr (see Chapter 7). They even have their very own villain—Mao's widow, Chiang Ching, demoted from cultural arbiter and censor to the humiliating official role of Enemy of Women's Liberation.

As Eileen realized when she tried to complete her personal research projects, the "freedoms" of China are quite limited. When Eileen asked questions about herbal medicine and acupuncture, she found that her family and the former colleagues of her father were unanimous in questioning: "Why do you want to know?" When they learned that Eileen was pursuing her own personal plans, that she had *chosen* a career in medicine, and that she was interested in making use of Chinese medical traditions, they did not praise her for this wish to follow her Chinese heritage. Instead, they were shocked by her "self-interest" in trying to determine her own future ("But what does your father say?"). One of the older professors even commented that he was afraid she had picked up Western habits of "petty bourgeois individualism."

My experiences, both in Canton and out in Kwangtung Province, included many examples of the ways in which the women of my family had improved their position since my mother's girlhood. But often the cause of this seemed to be better economic conditions in general rather than an improvement of their lot as women. I also found that single, younger women still enjoy much less freedom than do most wives and especially those traditionally sharp-tongued old ladies, the grannies.

Mao Tse-tung spoke of the "four thick ropes" that used to bind women. All Chinese peasants were "dominated" by three systems: political, clan, and religious authority. Women were dominated by a fourth—the authority of their husbands. Mao's ideas, however, did not become official policy until the Marriage Law of 1950, followed by the Constitution of 1954, in which women gained equal rights with men in all areas of cultural, political, economic, and social life.

One of my great-grandmothers and two of the elder aunts were "bound" in a more literal sense. They were victims of an old custom, in which mothers used to bind a small girl's feet tightly, with toes turned under, so that she would one day be a "desirable" bride, for men of the time greatly admired the ideal "dainty" foot that to us seems so grossly deformed. (A friend of my mother's now wears shoes specially constructed to conceal the ugliness that for so long was considered exquisitely beautiful).

I have no firsthand knowledge of the more widespread form of bondage—real slavery, which persisted right up to the beginnings of the People's Republic of China. One of Eileen's scholar friends in Peking showed her a contract written in terms that resemble those for indentured servants brought to America from Europe. Conditions were as terrible as those of black slaves in the South, and Chinese slaves were primarily women.

The document Eileen saw records a slave sale less than forty years ago, in Tibet, where the custom persisted longer than in other parts of China. I have read about slaves in China more than three thousand years ago. There was even a custom of burying live slaves with their dead masters. Yet I cannot imagine the kindly refugee lamas I have met in California being guilty of this practice. I also find it hard to believe that a child of my mother's generation could actually have been sold for fifty silver dollars—a transaction that included a refund guarantee in case the girl ran off or committed suicide.

Many of the slaves were children of poor families, whose parents sold them to wealthy landowners. Some Westerners have been told that these children were being trained as servants and that they were raised in relative comfort, but the available evidence suggest quite different conditions. Very few of the child slaves enjoyed any comfort or security, or experienced the luxuries that Japanese girls sold into prostitution by impoverished farming families found in the pleasure quarters of their country.

Even the most skeptical foreigner finds it difficult to dismiss all the evidence of slavery as Chinese propaganda. There are still many individuals, including thousands who are hostile to the current regime and now live in the United

States or Hong Kong, who can give eyewitness accounts of twentieth-century horrors—flogging of slaves with steel spring whips, near starvation, and harsh treatment. There are also records of slaves being tortured in ways as terrible as those of the Spanish Inquisition.

Eileen agrees that today's women are no longer household slaves. On the other hand, neither of us believes the recent travelers' tales claiming that fathers cook the dinner on mama's committee meeting night, or that old uncles have taken over all the "mothering" of the babies in communal nurseries and the sewing and laundry at neighborhood service centers. The centers do not "free" women from household tasks. Men and women working there provide valuable services for the job holders of both sexes.

According to contemporary theory in China, if the wife works late, the husband often prepares supper. From what I saw, in practice *both* of them are usually working late or attending committee meetings, and then both "eat out" (that is, at the canteen—his or hers—not in a fancy restaurant). Whenever schedules permitted the women in my family to be at home in the evening, it was the women who did the work. And just as older uncles do in California, the men liked to sit and puff on their pipes or discuss the performance of the factory's football team. Meanwhile, it was my aunts and girl cousins who set to work in the kitchen or cleared the table or scurried around to the market—even though in every case the women had put in just as many hours at school or job as the men.

Surely my Canton relations are not the only family in the whole of China still following this traditional pattern. On this point, friends who have visited China in groups cannot help me. They have been sheltered by the Travel Service or sequestered in hotels. Other Chinese-American friends with family in China commented, "It's just like the

United States. Why should men do the dishes if the women are willing to?"

One of Eileen's Shanghai uncles complained: "Nowadays, husbands have to fix breakfast for their wives." If they do, it is surely only because the wife (like my aunt) is out doing predawn marketing. I looked in vain for Chinese fathers pushing baby carriages, as men do in Denmark. Nor did I see fathers carrying babies in a backpack, as young fathers do in California—in spite of the traditional Chinese method of strapping a baby to its mother's back while she worked in the fields or aboard a boat.

A woman demanding that her husband assume equal shares of the household work soon finds that she is in trouble. The busybodies of the neighborhood committee are always willing to step in and arbitrate domestic squabbles. A neighbor of Eileen's aunt had tried to put her husband to work in the family kitchen. The committee ladies—alerted by the woman's outraged neighbors—called her in for some "criticism." At subsequent meetings, various women (including some of Eileen's relations) lectured the woman on her "poor attitude" and tried to correct her "faulty thinking." There was no question of women clumping together in this instance. They rallied around to denounce her "bad" political attitude—she was reminded that her treatment of her husband resembled that of a landlord browbeating a servant.

How "equal," then, are the partners in a modern Chinese marriage? Again, Eileen's conversations with her family in Shanghai confirm my own observations about the women of the Canton family and fellow workers in Kwangtung Province. There are some regional differences, of course, as there are in other countries, and among Eileen's sophisticated city connections there were even two women who sounded as though they had been reading

Western publications on the women's liberation movement.

But the words usually have different meanings. Eileen's relatives speak from the traditions of wealthy families, where the principal wife was absolute mistress of a home courtyard that often included more than twenty buildings, reception rooms for foreign and for Chinese guests, separate quarters for each of the concubines, rooms for servants, and storehouses for such wealth as rice and silk. The wife controlled domestic finances, and often "managed" her husband—at least on home territory—although in many cases their private relationship was one of affection and respect.

According to the official word out of the PRC, families like this no longer exist. It is true that none of Eileen's family can keep servants now. But under the system of economic reorganization in the 1950's, they apparently kept quite a bit of capital and quite a few possessions. They maintain a low profile and have to serve on committees and work for small salaries just like everyone else, but they show no signs of being discriminated against, of having their past wealth regarded as a kind of leprosy among their neighbors. And, unlike the young neighbor in Canton, who seemed untroubled at the thought of not following his family's medical tradition, two of Eileen's cousins were planning to become obstetricians, just like their grandmother and several of the aunts.

The institution of marriage has changed drastically even since these aunts were young. Arranged marriages were the custom then, although neither in Eileen's family nor in mine could we find one of those legendary brides who did not even see the husband until her wedding day. Among my rural connections, the couple rarely knew each other well, but in the small communities where they lived, they had usually at least glimpsed one another working in the fields.

By the time she got married, a peasant woman was already experienced in overcoming obstacles—including survival in a world where poor parents would just as soon let a sick girl baby die as go to the expense of raising her. Then there was the difficulty of finding a compatible partner, not someone who would please the girl (although she was expected to give full satisfaction to the stranger who was her husband), but one who would graciously accept her inevitable shortcomings—provided, of course, that the couple's horoscopes were compatible.

The twelve-animal zodiac was only one of many superstitions that controlled my rural ancestors. This complicated system matched partners according to the animal year of their birth, decreeing, for instance, "Two horses cannot live in the same stable." Even if the horoscopes were satisfactory, there were other customs and superstitions surrounding marriage—and these could even lead already hard-up families into bankruptcy, as they tried to provide the obligatory red money packets, gold ornaments for the bride, suitable costumes for all concerned, and a marriage feast costing more than an entire year's food supply.

Modern Chinese brides may well forego ceremonies entirely—although in California Chinese families still like to serve the appropriate dishes at lavish banquets, and to send out "felicitous" red-and-gold invitations. But the absence of wedding rings and the custom of women retaining their maiden names are part of a tradition that goes back to pre-Communist days.

As I had discovered in the park, young-marrieds forego such Western indulgences as a honeymoon. I sometimes wondered if today's brides do not perhaps lead a life as austere—and as hedged with restrictions—as they would have done forty years ago. A woman of my mother's generation often had to marry too young. Now the problem is reversed, and women must wait until they are about twenty-six (men are encouraged to wait until they are twenty-nine or thirty). Instead of having to marry for economic or for "family" reasons, couples today have to be sure that they please the State or at least their watchful fellow workers and the stern committees. Whenever I tried to talk to the young lathe operators or field workers about marriage expectations— when they would get married, where they would find a part- ner—they all seemed as uncomprehending as when I asked them about their "choice" of jobs.

I would have assumed that somehow "love would find a way" and that human nature could not be quite so drasti- cally suppressed. But there are powerful old Chinese taboos operating in the area of sex, and Western romantic notions of love and marriage are not supposed to be among the prerequisites for a sound relationship. Although many pas- sionate love lyrics and romantic stories and dramas have been written throughout past centuries, Chinese attitudes toward the relationship between husband and wife often seem to be entirely without the love and romance that American women associate with getting married.

Even among modern young Chinese-Americans, bonds of friendship and caring are often more important than sexual passion. Chinese parents raise their children not to be in a hurry to make love before marriage. I am much too casual in my relationships to suit my parents—or even Cousin Eileen—but my Western friends are always sur- prised when I am not quite as eager as they are to score. And I would never discuss my sex life with my sisters—or even with most of my friends.

I would have liked to talk to the girls of the commune. It would have been pleasant to walk through the Kwang-

tung fields or to have a companion for the movie nights—
there were many attractive girls. In fact, the good clean life
seemed to have produced some real beauties, with fine-
textured complexions and glossy hair (women in China do
not wear makeup, and there is nothing resembling our
Western cosmetics industry). But even if I had been able to
overcome the unspoken prohibition against being alone
with anyone of the opposite sex, it would not have occurred
to me to venture anything as intimate as a kiss.

To the young workers I met, our Western habits of dating, petting, and premarital sex seem as barbaric as the old
custom of foot binding. Several friends who have attempted
to make out with cousins or friends of the family during
their Kwangtung visits have reported that the result was
nothing but trouble. Unlike some Asian countries, where
romance with an American is seen as a ticket to United
States citizenship and a new life filled with automated luxuries, the Chinese girls seem to be much like our long-ago
ancestors—convinced that China is best, still the center of
the universe. Some told me how sorry they felt for various
relatives who had been shipped to California as young
brides (although I felt more sorry myself for the brides who
had to stay on in China while young husbands went to the
United States, worked on railroads, and sent home money
—sometimes finding a second wife in America).

Late in 1977, as an odd aftereffect of the overthrow of
the Gang of Four, according to my uncle, some of the rural
doctors arranged special programs of sex education for
their patients. The government published some pamphlets
on sex and birth control, too—in one province, it was the
first booklet with details of human reproduction that had
been available for twenty years. The advice offered by most
of the barefoot doctors who conducted some classes was not
much beyond the information given to elementary-school

students in the United States. And I saw one sports journal that included a piece you wouldn't have found in Western magazines fifty years ago: an article assuring girls that menstruation is not "dirty"—and they should not drink vinegar as a way of stopping it.

But group pressure against extramarital or premarital sex continues. I don't really believe that one of my friends saw "roadside chickens" (prostitutes) in Canton a few weeks ago. The couples strolling in the parks or sharing an umbrella at the zoo may occasionally hold hands, but there is no sex, no kissing and petting. These couples seem to me to be unnaturally content with the traditional restraints. They are part of a cultural scene that regards the restraint as quite natural and they say, "Of course no one gets married in their early twenties."

In modern China, girls are expected to be virgins at the time of their marriage, just as they were in past centuries. Strong social (group) pressures obviously make it difficult for them to be alone anywhere, the government system of travel permits makes it impossible for boys and girls to take trips together, and there are very few opportunities for an intimate relationship when all activities involve groups, and these groups are frequently segregated by sex (as in production teams, where I saw the girls competing against boys, and in many sports events).

One of my cousins told about some of the difficulties. A friend in their food-processing plant was actually found tucked away in a corner with a girl. What happened? A committee to the rescue, of course! The guilty couple was subjected to "severe criticism," getting off lightly. (Another worker who was caught with a married colleague had been immediately sent away, and there was a rumor that he had been assigned to one of the mysterious "rural labor camps" that sound to me like a Chinese version of Siberia.)

Did the couple at Cousin's plant show further signs of "bad attitude"? Certainly not! Their fellow workers continually delivered minilectures on "behaving immodestly." And just to make sure, Cousin said: "Of course we watched them very carefully all the time, to make sure that they did not do such a thing again. . . ." A system of worker-spies imposing a puritanical code? No wonder that the Chinese say, "We have no problem with illegitimate births," and claim that venereal diseases have been eradicated.

Clearly the "liberation" of women in China includes nothing resembling our Western sexual freedoms. The new freedoms were established in the Marriage Law of April 30, 1950, and described as "freedom to marry for men and women" (that is, without the earlier tyranny of arranged marriages, which emphasized family considerations). Mao had already stated through the Provisional Marriage Regulations of Kiangsi Soviet Republic (January 28, 1931) that "free choice should be the basic principle of marriage." In 1950, the law further decreed: "One wife to one husband."

With the stipulation "one wife" Mao was referring to the former custom of keeping concubines. When my friends in the United States come across this word, their usual response is a giggling assumption that the term means something akin to "mistress"—or perhaps (if they have watched old movies) a woman between Mata Hari and a gangster's girl friend. They assume that the concubine is someone not quite "nice" and definitely outside the law.

In China, however, a concubine had a clearly defined role and her own special place within the established social order. A bride in Old China (pre-1949) had one major function—to produce a son who would carry on the family name. Among the wealthier families, if the wife failed to produce an heir, it was she—not her husband—who went out and selected a suitable concubine.

As one of Eileen's aunts put it: "After all, if I have to live in the same courtyard with her for so many years, I want to make sure that he has someone I will like for a friend."

The "second wife" (and sometimes a third, if the family had sufficient wealth to support her) was legal in China (as in Hong Kong, until a few years ago). The concubine was a pragmatic solution to the problems of inheritance and family responsibility. The concubine in even a middle-level family had her own separate quarters, but she always ranked below the principal wife.

Eileen and I both regard the system as intolerable. Yet our aunts talk about it quite calmly. "Oh, yes," says Eileen's Auntie Chu, "I remember how difficult it was to find a suitable person. . . ."

Nowadays city couples in particular seem more concerned about limiting their family size than in producing a son. The national policy of late marriage is a form of population control, and Eileen even discovered that the women in some areas have to consult their work committees to see what the current quota is for maternity leave before they start a family. "If all the women had their babies at once, think of the disruption in production schedules," she was told.

My country family seem selfish to the Canton aunts because they are raising a family larger than the approved two-child ideal. But I found that there is a rather amusing sales resistance to government slogans out in the country. They are unimpressed by success stories of ideal families. My aunt was even so outspoken as to say that she would rather have nine children than nine thousand *jin* of grain. (This is in reference to one much-quoted inspirational piece of prosterilization literature, describing a group of women whose willingness to be sterilized was rewarded with their

own communal field and—when that produced an un-
usually high yield of grain—even more land, for even
greater yields.)

In the past, large families were a form of social security and old-age pension. Now the government has taken
over the children's former role, providing old-age benefits
and "five guarantees."

The five guarantees include food, clothing, fuel, burial,
and the education of children through middle school. In the
commune, old folk without close family to look after them
are guaranteed cooking oil, firewood, and grain, as well as
medical care and what my granny described as "pocket
money." There are supposed to be rules about retirement
age (usually between sixty and sixty-eight), but from what
I saw all the oldsters take pride in continuing on the job—
even if all they can do is hand-carry a few containers of
water during a drought or put in an hour or two in the communal nursery. Some take on quite ambitious "side jobs,"
like the old ladies I heard about who got together on a
weaving project—and used the money to pay for their brigade's new peanut thresher.

Women may have been liberated from many earlier
bonds, and they have certainly proved that they are able
to work in all the areas previously reserved for men. But
this does not mean that China is one vast unisex society.
For instance, women are still quite pleased to be praised for
special talents—in embroidery, in medicine, and even as
"sympathetic" members of the police force (where they
routinely put in after-duty hours warning old grannies
about the dangers of coal-gas poisoning, or they work with
neighborhood committees to combat litter and discourage
would-be criminals).

Women do not seem to mind having some "special protections," detailed in Chinese laws and in the instruction

manuals given to young medical workers. These protections are designed to make proper allowances for biological differences. In addition to their paid maternity leave (about fifty days in the commune, slightly longer in the city, and additional time off for the birth of twins or if there are complications), women have work-schedule modifications during menstruation and pregnancy. Mothers also have time off from their jobs to nurse babies, but this is not exactly a holiday—just the extra time needed to walk from workbench or field to the factory or commune nursery, where they efficiently suckle the babies and then go right back to the job.

No Chinese woman stays home to raise a family. They think that is a lazy habit of the "decadent" West. But one of the few times that I heard my companions in the rural dormitory laugh (instead of expressing simple disapproval of Western habits) was when I described to them the Swedish welfare regulations that permit the *husband* to take paid "maternity" leave—staying home to keep house and bottle-feed the infant, while the wife goes back to her office or other job. They applauded my tale of house husbands as "humorous American storytelling."

Women have certainly come a long way from the time when rural superstitions blamed them even for such natural calamities as drought (said to indicate the mountain god's displeasure when they appeared in certain fields). Now they have overcome old superstitions and pioneered a new occupation—barefoot or "little" doctor. "Barefoot" refers to their work in the southern rice fields, which are flooded through most of the growing season. The two million barefoot doctors now include many men, although my friends in the Kwangtung production team were mostly girls under twenty.

The services they provide are more varied and require

more skills than we include in the concept of Western paramedics. I sampled their herbal medicines and watched them at work, but it was Eileen who obtained more information when she talked to Shanghai relatives about the possibility of studying traditional medicine in China. Her family vetoed the idea, but they were all agreed that barefoot doctors and new neighborhood clinics have improved the health of workers in every part of the country.

With only six months of formal training, the barefoot doctor takes first-aid kit and treatment manual to an assignment in the fields. Duties include simple acupuncture and moxibustion treatments (the application of a burning substance to the skin) as well as immunizations, traditional herbal prescriptions and the use of modern (Western) pharmaceuticals. As a public-health worker, the barefoot doctor meets with groups to discuss family planning, diet, sewage management, and basic hygiene. Some of the time is spent in the brigade's clinic, referring patients needing more specialized treatment to province hospitals, or doing follow-ups on recently discharged hospital patients—usually working under the supervision of staff with advanced medical training.

My Kwangtung aunt also mentioned several cases in which the barefoot doctor cleaned house and took care of the laundry. But no matter how hard I tried, I simply could not imagine an American doctor who would be willing to make house calls and would then also brew tea for the patient and spend a few minutes more washing out the patient's pajamas!

When I thanked the barefoot doctor who prescribed my herbal brew, and said how thoughtful she was to make a follow-up visit, she apologized for being only a very new doctor. It was a pity that I could not meet her predecessor, who would be coming home on vacation soon. . . . Had I actually discovered a New China occupation in which workers enjoy holidays? No. This young doctor was doing additional study in the provincial medical school, using semester breaks to keep in touch back home, where she held classes for younger colleagues and hoped someday to practice in the brigade hospital.

Our brigade included eighty barefoot doctors, three midwives, a clinic, and on-the-spot health stations, so that no production-team member was ever very far from competent medical care. Many of the young doctors I met were expecting to continue doing double duty as medical workers and in the fields or factories until they reach retirement age. Others have already left for more conventional, advanced professional training. One has become an orthopedic surgeon.

There were many women in medicine before Mao issued his directive emphasizing rural health care. Like members of Eileen's family, women were often obstetrician-gynecologists (a feminine monopoly in China). Yet some of the earliest barefoot doctors brought medical skills to a group that previously regarded working women with horror—the fishermen off the South China coast. The first women doctors allowed aboard their boats were all daughters of fishermen, and some were only seventeen years old. Now they do double duty at sea, carrying medical equipment, but with primary assignments as fishing-boat mates or mechanics. Some of this pioneer group have already been selected for further study at Kwangtung Provincial College of Traditional (that is, Chinese) Medicine. One now practices in a hospital.

Eileen had hoped to study traditional Chinese medicine, just as I had hoped to share commune life. Her family claimed that the medical schools were too crowded to accommodate their foreign cousin—although she suspected

A barefoot doctor carefully weighs out the herbs and various exotic ingredients used in traditional Chinese prescriptions. But she can also prescribe the same antibiotics and other drugs available in the West.

that the real reason might have been the chaotic state of professional schools. Emphasis on physical labor had persuaded both of us that professional training had been almost eliminated from the Chinese scene. And some announcements from China in the fall of 1977 suggest that the authorities themselves were recognizing that the old, rigorous medical training ought to be restored.

In the past—when her aunts were in medical school—professional training in China was no different from that in the West. It included specialization after five or six years of academic training—at Chungshan, thirty-six courses before students could see a live patient! During the years of the Cultural Revolution, training was shortened to perhaps three years of combined study and rural practice. But too many medical schools had the same admissions policies for both men and women as other colleges and universities, with the usual reverse discrimination (the more professionals, intellectuals, landlords, or rich peasants in your ancestry, the poorer your chances of admission).

Her family thought that the best Eileen could hope for would be a return to China after she qualifies professionally in the United States or Canada—as many foreign doctors have already come to study acupuncture or herbal remedies, usually for only two or three weeks. The best they could do was to arrange several sessions of hospital observation, in which the ancient art of acupuncture was used (supplemented with electrical charges) for anesthesia in various surgical procedures.

The Chinese eagerness to display patients and surgeons for public viewing—even when the observers are not in the medical professions—struck Eileen as strange. But it was an experience that she says she would gladly repeat a hundred times. . . .

The paradox of modern Chinese medicine at the professional level—and it affected men and women alike—was that there are superb research institutes, especially in the fields of burn medicine and cancer studies, which were able to maintain high standards in spite of the falling off at the graduate schools. Yet the general standard of health care—and of women's professional accomplishments—remained high.

China's striving for the "good Communist life" does not include the Western obsession with women "getting to the top in a man's field." People seem to take for granted the way in which a neighborhood lightbulb enterprise escalates into a complex temperature-controlled diffusion furnace factory, whereas an American home-dressmaking operation that becomes an important part of the garment industry makes headlines. In China, they often desex their success stories and stress not a woman's achievement, but a general socioeconomic gain (as when a Shanghai waif becomes a crack pilot).

But when Mao Tse-tung made his much-quoted statement that "women hold up half the sky," he was clearly liberating them from more than two thousand years of masculine (Confucian) superiority, as well as from the harsh bonds of their years of actual slavery. . . .

II

AFTERTHOUGHTS

HOMEWARD BOUND at last, the train to Hong Kong traveled back from Canton over the same tracks. The view from the windows would never again look quite as it did twelve weeks earlier, when I went looking for the China of my father's memories.

The Chinese traditions of which I was so proud seem to be better preserved in the United States than in the People's Republic of China. However much I admired the forward-looking modern Chinese people, it was disappointing to find that the literary classics, more than a thousand years of poetry, and the ancient arts of China were less familiar to my cousins than to a freshman class of Western college students who had never set foot on the Asian mainland.

It was disconcerting to realize how little Eileen and I still know about China—in spite of the fact that every possible activity seems to have been set up as spectator sport for visiting Western tourists, with showcase communes, factories, even prisons (Shanghai) all part of the three-star production, even front-row seats for an intimate view of surgery done with acupuncture anesthesia.

Like many other Western visitors, I often found myself looking at the modern Chinese scene from a negative perspective: the constraints that I found intolerable; the monotony of "group-speak" and activities en masse; the lack of the comforts that I had taken for granted. But my family in China helped me to understand that each of the seeming flaws could also be looked at quite differently. Often what seemed bad to me was good in their eyes. They take the positive approach, seeing how much today's life has improved in comparison with past hardships.

I could see only the burdens imposed by the various time-consuming and restrictive committees that organize every aspect of Chinese life from conception to burial. My relatives who sit on such committees see only the benefits of committee-set production schedules, wages, accident compensation. They point to the benefits in case of fire or earthquake from committee-organized disaster relief, the "fairness" of committees' selecting workers to be given further education or new job assignments.

During my weeks in China, slogans and statistics designed to support these claims of a splendid new life often drove me to distraction. Even art is reduced to statistics: "Ten thousand works of art by coal miners and industrial workers of Yangchuan in one three-year period." No matter where I went, I continually found that students or computer programmers or dam builders were eager to overwhelm me with the facts and figures of their country's good points— usually with an enthusiasm that outdid the maddest fantasies of any hometown boosters or American chambers of commerce.

Recurrent magical numbers and heroic accomplishments numbed my senses. The people moved mountains—

seven gullies and eight ridges at Tachai. They accomplished miracles in the face of "seven natural calamities." Their animals multiplied with biblical fertility: seven donkeys, one pig, and eight oxen rapidly became four hundred animals. But I cannot grasp such wonders as the Shashiyu Production Brigade's "five winters and six springs" during which members walked "ten thousand *li* to carry one thousand loads of soil to reclaim each single *mu* of land" (a project aided by out-of-town friends and relatives arriving with picnic hampers filled not with food but with loads of dirt from more fertile fields).

On the other hand, I could see that in several areas modern China seems to have some suggestions for the West. We would not care to elevate labor to an act of heroism, as they do. Yet I could appreciate a system that does not continually place "head" above "hand," and that admires both the promise of youth (Mao's "The Future Belongs to You!") and the accomplishments of age (the ways in which people we would describe as experts or managerial staff constantly consulted "experienced" workers and "old" farmers).

Our concern with the environment is still imperfect in the West. In China the frugal habits of my ancestors are now applied to contemporary problems of pollution and public health. It would be easy to mock that poem (Mao's "Farewell to the God of Plague") celebrating the elimination of a snail-borne disease (schistosomiasis), yet surely the end of that scourge of the rice fields merited celebration. Public educational campaigns also seem to have eliminated social diseases, such as TB and VD, and China's program of preventive medicine (with the cooperation of neighborhood committees, soldiers, and schoolchildren) is one that many people in our inner cities would appreciate.

In combating pollution, the Chinese have good ideas.

I heard of one plant where workers are now breeding gold-fish in cleaned-up water from an oil refinery. At another, they reduced the output of solid wastes from 12,800 tons to 250—and produced twenty-four new products out of the residues. They have also recognized that clean air means something more than the elimination of smoke and smog. They have swept the air clean of flies and their campaigns to "Fight Disease!" involve everyone from grandpa to tod-dler—all doing their bit to sweep and swat the menaces of fleas, lice, mosquitoes, ticks, and granary beetles. Nor do the Chinese pollute the environment with pesticides. Often, instead of using pesticide strips, for instance, they prefer home-brewed remedies, such as a bait of crushed tobacco leaves and rice gruel.

The Chinese have also done well in the field of indus-trial medicine. The Shenyang Labor Health Research In-stitute, built in 1960, is studying occupational hazards, inspecting working conditions, and suggesting technical im-provements (such as dust-free methods of grinding, or methods of radiation detection and shielding), identifying industrial poisons, and so on. The institute regularly sends researchers to conduct courses on industrial hazards at fac-tories and mines. Research teams are sent to work in mines or industrial plants (instead of sending them just to observe or to collect data, as in the West). Sometimes this system produces fringe benefits, such as a herbal treatment for silicosis developed from a home remedy popular with the coal miners.

The Chinese have also been pioneers in fuel conserva-tion, creating the world's first central heating system—the *k'ang*. They were using these brick platforms at a time when Europeans were still making do with smoky open wood fires, and the *k'ang* is still in widespread use (especially in the north). It is a pleasant sitting area by day, with warm sleeping space for an entire family at night: and frequently its only "fuel" is otherwise wasted heat from cooking. Padded coats play a part in fuel conservation too, although often in the past there were countless people too poor to own one. Generally, though, the Chinese today still prefer to put on extra padded garments for warmth, instead of having the wastefully overheated homes and offices of America.

I doubt, though, that we in America would want to follow the Chinese in going back to the gaslight era. In some rural areas the Chinese have now devised a home heater that uses all kinds of waste materials, fermented with water, and then piped to kitchen stoves and lamps (equivalent to a one hundred-watt bulb). Even the residue from these contraptions is salvaged, raked out for fertilizer. I even heard of plans to build larger models that will power generators and pumps.

But are all the marvels in modern China really to be credited to the regimes of Mao and Hua? My knowledge of Chinese traditions and history suggests otherwise. A Western visitor ignorant of this past may be overwhelmed by vast irrigation projects, as when the PRC announces that 3 million men and women have moved 185 million cubic meters of earth ("equivalent to building the Panama Canal in eight months," say the boosters, adding that "many of the workers accepted only a daily ration of rice for their labors").

I think of earlier achievements, such as the first attempts to control the Yellow River, back in 2100 B.C. The Great Yu of that time was a hero to match Mao's moderns. He was so devoted to his engineering work that he did not go home, or even see his new bride, for thirteen years. There were two pioneering hydraulic engineers—Li Ping and his son—two thousand years ago. Today's irrigation and flood-control projects include impressive statistics of the Red

Flag Canal. Yet the Chinese were doing this sort of thing a thousand years before Europeans set foot in America. They were making canals and flood-control projects as early as 1000 B.C., and the Grand Canal from Hangchow to Loyang was built in the sixth century A.D.

History repeats itself. The new Republic takes pride in its accomplishments and repudiates the past. China's first emperor, Ch'in Shih Huang-ti (246–210 B.C.) is credited with the Great Wall, vast irrigation projects, a unified system of writing, scientific advances, a legal code. Like Mao, the emperor rejected the teachings of the past (including Confucius). He burned the classics in 221 B.C. and persecuted scholars who favored the past. He wanted to "purify" the country. Will Mao one day be similarly labeled as "a tyrant-dictator, who used forced labor"? Other soldiers and leaders of peasant armies have staged rebellions in China, and often they were guilty of the same abuses as the "villains" they had just ousted.

Life in modern China is not always quite as far from past traditions as the Communists claim. The elitist Confucian code is officially rejected. Yet Confucian ethics seem to underlie many modern attitudes. Confucian ideas of male dominance are out of fashion, but the Chinese are still affected by his ideas on the relationship between people and state (resembling that of an extended family) and concepts of group responsibility.

Often in China, past traditions and new ways coexist. Mao said: "The past serves the present." The rural worker uses a primitive harness or hoe at one minute and a twenty-horsepower tractor the next (and has often forged parts of that tractor himself). Workers spread winter wheat on the streets of Peking for some unconventional "threshing" by passing trucks. Yet even in the most remote Autonomous Regions, where some workers still hoe and herd as they did a thousand years ago, there are now mechanical threshers for rice and peanuts, sophisticated scientific monitoring equipment, and complex irrigation projects. Ancient poetic forms denounce modern villains. A new fifteen-thousand-ton ship is launched to the sound of traditional music. And even Chairman Mao's last volumes of posthumously published essays are welcomed to the bookshops with traditional gongs and cymbals.

Often the traditions have been reconstituted for the benefit of modern men and women—as in the beautiful parks and lakes inherited from long-ago mandarins and monks. Would that our inner cities were so blessed with recreational space and that volunteers would pitch in to help with the construction (as they did in Canton's Liuhua —Stream of Flowers—Park, with its lovely causeway across the water).

In medicine, this use of the past is a national policy. "Traditional," or Chinese, herbs and folk remedies and Western pharmaceuticals, Chinese acupuncture and the most sophisticated machines of modern medicine are used side by side (and often for the same illness, and on the same patient). Western visitors see contradictions in these combinations of ancient and modern. Yet in many cases the old "superstitions" have produced excellent cure rates, and often the old ways can be justified in terms of modern scientific knowledge. One scholar in Hanoi even went so far as to see in the ancient theories of *yin* and *yang* evidence that the Chinese identified the adrenal glands a thousand years before Western doctors knew their function. European medical opinion began to acknowledge some of the benefits of acupuncture (in the treatment of arthritis and rheumatism) early in the nineteenth century. Recent American visitors have seen the old needles augmented with electric currents and used for complication-free anesthesia. . . .

I have to admit that my limited experiences of Chinese herbalists and home remedies back in San Francisco had not quite prepared me for some of the more exotic treatments that I encountered among my rural relations. I share with my Caucasian friends a disbelief at some of the items listed solemnly in the accepted manuals of traditional medicine: animal bones, the "moltings" of snake and cicada, pulverized scorpion and centipede, silkworm debris of various kinds—even "hearth-dried" toad for leg ulcers, bat droppings, and in the family medicine book that the country granny showed me, a mysterious "fungus scraped from coffin lids."

A cancer cure that begins "Take one live frog" sounds like something out of Macbeth rather than officially accepted treatment (it is wrapped in dirt, toasted or baked, pulverized, and taken in three doses per day). Yet as Eileen reminded me, the lowly frog has all sorts of valuable substances tucked away in his ugly body. In fact, the United States' National Institute of Health sent an expedition to South America to collect jungle frogs, hoping that the venom might prove valuable in surgery and in the treatment of heart disease).

It is easy to get a cheap laugh from the "superstitions" of folk medicine or cures suggested by physicians hundreds of years ago (at a time when the doctor was not allowed to see—let alone examine—his female patients). But those "quaint" old fellows seem to have been aware of psychosomatic illness at a time when most Europeans were still burning witches. Their system does not quite coincide with Western psychiatry's, but it does include subtle distinctions of "seven emotions"—anger, fear, joy, pensiveness, sadness, sorrow, worry—linked to various physical symptoms (they used the expression "injury by the seven emotions").

As I found in my village stay, traditional medicine not

only works—it is well suited to the distances and the conditions of the People's Republic of China. It makes maximum use of available materials and avoids Western dependency upon expensive and complex equipment. And the Chinese have realized something that we are only just beginning to think about: a caring individual (such as the barefoot doctor) can often accomplish more than all the specialists and machines of twentieth-century medicine.

Much of the past has been discarded with good cause. Surely everyone must be glad to see the end of bound feet, the final abolition of slavery, the passing of tyrannical mandarins and greedy landlords. It is good to see the end of superstitions that prevented women from working in the fields and on the fishing boats (lest they offend the gods of mountain or sea). A modern engineer is probably more reliable than a geomancer in deciding where to sink a well. . . .

Looking at the present, however, can be as confusing as the Chinese scene was to gullible travelers seven hundred years ago. Many visitors are as overwhelmed by the smiling faces as by the impressive statistics. But what of the 900 million faces that we do not see, and the facts and figures that are not among those officially released wonder tales of the People's Republic of China?

Part of the problem today lies in the impossibility of traveling independently and of communicating with people whose speech—and ideas—must make us depend on interpreters. Even among my family, I could not be sure how much of what was said and done resulted from my presence, from their desire (and mine) to show a good face. Will my cousins, when I am no longer within earshot, turn to cursing their government, stealing from their neighbors, committing adultery with their seemingly desexed co-workers? Even the tidbits that Granny read aloud from her newspaper's court reports did not tell me just how much dissent and punishment goes on behind those protective walls, and in the compartmentalized world that keeps so many workers segregated in social and intellectual ghettos.

Occasionally, my experience as a Chinese-American helped me to see behind the gestures of official spokesmen. After the Tangshan earthquake, for instance, when the area had been off limits to newspersons from the West, they cried: "Censorship!" After the local people had restored some sort of order to their lives, reporters were again allowed in—but they were told not to take photographs. They looked for sinister reasons to explain this prohibition. To me, they were already infringing on traditional Chinese practices—the reluctance to expose personal sorrow or discomfort to public display or record. (By contrast, the admission of visitors to operating rooms to observe acupuncture anesthesia and other techniques is not considered invasion of the patient's privacy but a proud display of Chinese surgical skills.)

I was sometimes puzzled by aspects of the modern Chinese scene. For instance, I liked the grand sound of Mao's peasant-artists "with hoe in one hand and brush in the other," and I admired the lively new paintings. But it was disappointing to realize how many of my relatives had *not* seen the treasures that have been so lavishly displayed for us in the West—even those works identified as "discoveries by peasant workers" in remote provinces. Cousin Wang patiently explained some of the difficulties of setting up traveling exhibits where distances are great and families do not go traveling about the country on sightseeing trips. But at least during the time of my visit, I would have been happier to discover more widespread opportunities for seeing ancient art treasures.

I had been inspired by traveling exhibitions of a princess's jade suit, ceramic camels and bronze horses and birds a thousand years old, ancient weapons uncorroded by time, reproductions of wall paintings in ancient tombs. It was exciting to read of "gallant peasant laborers" who set out to construct a pumping station, and found a 7,000-year-old settlement or discovered a 3,300-year-old copper-casting mill—or even animal-shaped pots made more than 7,000 years ago. Yet I found that no one in my family had been able to make the long journey to see these treasures. Only Uncle Wu and an aunt whose neighborhood sports team went to Peking have seen the splendid beasts that guard the Ming Tombs. In spite of such exhibits as those in Kwang-chow Museum (Zhenhai Tower), for many Chinese people the treasures remained as effectively buried as if they had still been underground with those life-sized pottery warriors and horses found by rural workers in Tang and Han burial sites.

I was disappointed that so much of my intellectual and cultural heritage seemed to be effectively hidden from sight in modern China. The scrolls of painting and poetry, the ancient manuscripts of philosophers and playwrights are found only on inaccessible university library shelves. Knowing no different, my cousins love their Five-Good Soldiers and read their Mao as they are taught to do. But I am sorry that Lao Tzu's mystic way (*Tao:* the mystic way or road) seems to have more followers in southern California than in southern China. On the other hand, Lao Tzu wrote in a typical contradiction: "Those who speak know nothing/ Those who know are silent." The poet Po Chü-yi retorted: "How is it, then, that Lao Tzu himself wrote a book of five thousand words?"

Perhaps I too should remain silent about what I saw and felt. As one French scholar observed a few years ago: "Chinese travelers are loquacious in inverse ratio to the amount of information they have." And the accounts that now come flooding from the cameras and pens and lips of China tourists remind me of Marco Polo's journal. Recorded by Rusticello, it now exists in 120 versions—all based on the same experience, the same words, but no two agreeing in all their details.

Ironically, too, in many ways we are still as ignorant—and as curious—as the earliest foreigners who visited Peking, those Roman musicians eighteen hundred years ago, Japan's seventh-century embassy, Roman Catholic missionaries in the thirteenth and fourteenth centuries. The words of the new-generation emissaries who have seen China for themselves are studied as eagerly as those earlier reports.

Past accounts described "the people of China," although the writers had only glimpsed stage-managed segments of the imperial court, just as our travelers today are ushered along prescribed routes. Today's visitors analyze the flaws and praise the virtues of the People's Republic of China after two weeks—or three days—of instant photography. Ignorant of the language, they confidently report on "life in China today," although everything they have seen or heard has been filtered through interpreters and sometimes gives the impression of being carefully posted or rehearsed.

Even when their knowledge of the language is better than mine, or they cover more miles than Eileen did, they still experience no more than a smudge on the map of China. We all know that it is dangerous to generalize, and I know how limited my family view of China seems. I never visited a northern farm. I have seen neither yurt nor cave house. I have not even seen the Great Wall. And my two weeks on a commune have little in common with the idyllic experiences of some Western visitors. I remember two weeks of utter exhaustion. They often seem to have spent more than half their "working" hours as tourists visiting other farms and factories.

Family reticences sometimes blocked my view of the local scene as effectively as any overprotective official guide from the China Travel Service. It was only after I was back at home, for instance, that I realized how much my relations had "spared" me. According to my mother, they did not want to "embarrass" me by telling me that they had to "register" their visitor's activities with the local committees, that they had to supply coupons for the rice and restaurant meals that I enjoyed, that some of the money my father sent them (and I begrudged) was diverted at the insistence of community-minded committee watchdogs, making sure that the group received a "fair" percentage of the individual's (private) gain.

Leaving Canton in 1977, I thought about the many kindnesses of my family. Granny's home remedies, Auntie's concern as I wandered about the streets, cousins and uncles trying to please me. Perhaps some of their actions were designed to make sure that I did not put them in a bad light when I returned to California—although even the most fulsome praises would not satisfy my Travel Service cousin. I have tried to protect their privacy by making changes in names and other details. But I wish I could thank them more adequately.

So at last I traveled home—to California, where we take spontaneity and freedom of action for granted. After listening to the Big Brother voices of loudspeakers and of committees proclaiming just who shall go working on the railroad and who is to go to the fields of rice or oil, what a relief it was to be going home—where I can turn on my own sound system and make my own choice of music and of time.

The Chinese themselves seem to like their world. I saw no signs of discontent among my family. And they are the ones who have to live there, after all. But for my part, the weeks of living in the New China have convinced me that a Chinese-American does not belong back in the ancestral village. I am happier to return home—to the United States —to my Golden Mountain, San Francisco.

INDEX

A

Abacus, use of, 90, 91, 96
Accidents, automobile, 62
Achievements, history of Chinese, 226
Acrobats, skill of, 84
Activities, Sunday, 68
Adult education, 148
Age and work, 52
Agriculture, workers in, 168
Ambition, lack of personal, 153
American-Chinese, problems of, 235
Apartment, typical city, 65
Artistic
   contributions, Chinese, 46
   expression on commune, 198
Artists, worker, 148
Arts
   ancient, neglect of, 222
   on the commune, 198
   political nature of, 86
   propaganda in the, 98
Athletes, lack of star system for, 159
Attitude
   to old age, 224
   to work, 120, 121
   to youth, 224
Austerity, standard of, 152
Authority symbols, 24
Automobile, automobiles
   accidents, handling, 62
   lack of private, 60
   pollution, 36

B

Barefoot doctors
   medicines of, 183
   methods of, 141
   role of, 217
   women as, 216
Bicycles
   number of, 185, 186
   use of, 60, 61
Big Character posters, 104, 105
Birth rate, control of, 214
Birthday observances, lack of, 214
Boat people, 25
Books and propaganda, 97
Border regulations, 28
Boredom, problem of, 66
Boy-girl relationships, 211
Bridge into China, walking the, 30
Brigades, commune, 174
Bureaucracy, Chinese, 26

C

Cafeterias, factory, 134
Calligraphy, art of, 94
Cameras, shortage of, 74

Canton
  clothing in, 37, 57
  foreigners in, 56
  housing in, 38
  at night, 82
  products, 128
  slums, 53
  streets of, 36, 48
Canton Cultural Park, 82
Career choice, lack of, 120
Carts, pedal-power, 60
Censorship, self, 102
Central Institute for Nationalities, 110
Changes
  in China, sequence of, 45
  recent, 12
Children. *See also* Youth.
  behavior of, 72
  productive labor and, 93
Children's Railway, Harbin, 116
China Reconstructs, 12
Chinese-American, problems of, 235
Choice
  of career, restrictions on, 120
  restrictions on, 114, 115
  in school, lack of, 100
Classroom, typical, 192
Cleanliness
  of railway station, 30
  urban, 48
Clothing, Cantonese, 37
Committee, committees.
       See also Group.
  lane, 52
  neighborhood, 52
  street, 52
  system, decision by, 103
Commune, communes
  as agribusiness, 165
  bathing on, 167
  brigades in, 174
  closed nature of, 162
  creativity on, 198
  dormitory, 168
  efficiency, 176, 177
  entertainment, 195, 196
  evening activities, 168, 170
  hard labor on, 167, 171
  housing, 165
  ingenuity of, 178
  life, idealization of, 162
  living costs, 190
  privacy, lack of, 170

  production teams, 174
  regimentation on, 170
  scope of activities, 176, 177
  size, 165, 176
  sports on, 173
  system, origin of, 169
  toilets on, 170
  variety of, 177
  wages, 189
  and Western communes, contrast
       of, 163, 176
  work
    attitude to, 173
    day, 167
    pace, 166, 171
Communicating with people, difficulty
  in, 230
Community, closeness of work, 119
Competition, sports, 79
Concubines, role of, 213
Confucian ideas, influences of, 227
Conservation, fuel, 225
Consumer goods, shortages in, 63
Consumerism, lack of, 153
Contentment, basis of, 139
Cooperatives, early, 169
Cost, costs
  of living, commune, 190
  average, 132
Country work, variety of, 125
Craft skills, 129
Crime, urban, 51, 53
Cultural
  contributions, Chinese, 46
  Park, Canton, 82
  past, hidden, 231
  Revolution, 104
Cultures, minority, 111
Curriculum
  normal school, 93
  university, 102

                    D

Daily regimentation, 48
Dating customs, 211
Decisions, group, 118
Delinquency, urban, 53
Dialects, variations among, 23
Dictionary, use of Chinese, 23
Dim sum, 76
Discontent, lack of, 235
Discrimination, lack of ethnic, 110

Disease control, 224
  venereal, 213
Doctors. *See also* Medical,
      Medicines.
  barefoot
    medicines of, 183
    methods, 141
    use of, 217
    women as, 216
  women, 218
Dress in Canton, 57
Driver training, 61

E

Education. *See also* School,
      Universities.
  adult, 148
  professional, standards for, 113
  purpose of, 92
  sex, 211
  standards, concern about, 111
Entertainers, traveling, 196
Entertainment. *See also* Leisure
      activity.
  commune, 195, 196
Entry into China, problems of, 28
Ethnic discrimination, lack of, 110
Exercises, morning, 55
Exports, 135, 137

F

Factory, factories
  cafeterias, 134
  location of, 125
  lunches, 133
  overtime, 134
  textile, 127
  and universities, relationship of,
      109
  women's support of, 124
Family
  dinner, village, 181
  feelings about, 34
  gifts from overseas, 41
  life, village, 180
  relationships, 24
  women's role in, 216
Feet, binding girls', 204
Film, shortage of, 71
Fireworks, skill in, 161
Five-Good Soldier, 98

Five guarantees of security, 215
Folk medicines, 229
Food
  conformity in, 54
  festive, 39
  importance of, 39
  variety in, 39, 40
Foreigners
  in Canton, 56
  tours for, 64
Free time, lack of, 67, 140, 154
Freedom
  of choice, lack of, 114, 115
  to travel, lack of, 115
Fuel conservation, 61, 225
Furniture, old, 39

G

Gambling, Chinese fondness for, 28
Gang of Four, attacks on, 107
Gasoline conservation, 61, 225
Geography of China, 17, 44
Gifts from families overseas, 41
Ginseng, use of, 183
Girl-boy relationships, 211
Goods, consumer
  availability of, 63
  prices of, 63
Government, women in, 202
Group. *See also* Committee.
  activity
    preference for, 60
    prevalence of, 66
  decisions, 118
  tyranny, 121
Guarantees of security, five, 215

H

Han people, 45
Harbin Children's Railway, 116
Health
  care, 221
  costs, 132
History
  of achievements, 226
  study of, 97
Holidays, national, 151
Hong Kong
  ambivalence of, 25
  appearance of, 17
  atmosphere of, 18

harbor, 17
street scenes, 18
as transition to China, 18
view of, 22
Horoscopes in Old China, importance of, 209
Housework and women, 206
Housing
Cantonese, 38
job segregation in, 66
Humility, traditional, 124

I

Ice cream, 77
Ideographs, writing, 93
Idleness, attitude to, 172
Illegitimate births, low level of, 213
Imports, 137
Industrial medicine, 225
Industrialization
over-all, 136
rural, 125
Industry, industries
and profit factor, 125
rural, and local needs, 125
women and support for, 124
Inventions, worker, 140, 141
Isolation, tendency to, 28, 29

J

Job segregation in housing, 66
Jokes, political, 86
Junks, 19

K

Kai Tak Airport, 17
Kam Tin village, 25
Kuomintang, 81
Kwangtung Province, 26, 44

L

Labor
productive, and school children, 93
student, 115, 116
women's role in, 202
Lane committees, 52
Language, languages
complexities of, 21
variations in Chinese, 45

Laws, traffic, 62
Leisure activity
movies as, 156
restaurant meal as, 155
Literacy rate, 193
Literature, current, 193
Litter, level of, 50
Little Red Book, Mao's, 92
Living costs on commune, 190
Lunch, factory, 133
Luxury, denial of, 65

M

Magazines, contents of, 31
Mandarin speech, name of, 121
Mao
Little Red Book of, 92
as teacher, 92
Marriage
customs
changes in, 208
modern, 209
in Old China, 209
ideas on, 210
law, 213
May 7 schools, purpose of, 108
Meals, restaurant, 76, 155
Medical. *See also* Doctors, Medicine.
care, 221
training, 220
Medicine, medicines. *See also* Doctors, Medical.
of barefoot doctors, 183
folk, 229
industrial, 225
preventive, 224
rural, 182
Men and women, barriers between, 201
Middle Country name for China, 29
Minority, minorities
cultures, interest in, 111
role of, 111
treatment of, 44
Modernization, recent trends to, 12
Morning exercises, 55
Movies
changes in, 158
as leisure activity, 156
as propaganda, 156
Music
classic Chinese, 86

constant, 31
modern Chinese, 86
Western, 86

N

Name for China, Middle Country, 29
National holidays, 151
Natural resources, 137
Neighborhood committees, 52
New Territories, view of, 25
Newspapers
as propaganda, 160
publishing, 160
Night
Canton at, 82
safety, 82
Noise
pollution, 31
prevalence of, 81
Noodle shops, 58

O

Occupation, selection of, 116
Oil industry and workers, 144
Old
age, attitude to, 224
China, romantic view of, 24
Open-air shows, 84
Overseas, family gifts from, 41
Overtime, work, 134

P

Parades, 81
Parks
political, 80
prevalence of, 69
Peasant, connotation of word, 169
Pedal-power carts, 60
Peking University, 109
People
difficulty in communicating with,
230, 233
power as labor, 168
regional stereotypes in, 45
variations in Chinese, 44
People's Liberation Army, role of,
146
Pep talks, propaganda, 31
Personal ambition, lack of, 153
Photographer, public, 74

Pigs, importance of, 176
Pleasures, basis of, 139
Poetry, modern, 149
Political. *See also* Politics,
Propaganda.
arguments, absence of, 60
jokes, 86
parks, 80
posters, 75
rallies, 80, 81
Politics. *See also* Political,
Propaganda.
and the arts, 86
and movies, 156
in village life, 184
Pollution
automobile, 36
combating, 224
noise, 31
Polygamy in Old China, 214
Population control, 214
Ports, changes in, 135
Posters
Big Character, 104, 105
political, 75
Preventive medicine, 224
Prices of goods, 63
Privacy
on commune, lack of, 170
lack of general, 42, 153
Production teams, commune, 174
Professional education, standards
for, 113
Professors, re-education of, 108
Profit factor and industry, 125
Propaganda. *See also* Political,
Politics.
in the arts, 98
in books, 97
movies as, 156
newspapers as, 160
pep talks, 31
television as, 158
Public
photographer, 74
storyteller, 195
Publishing, quality of, 31

R

Races in China, variety of, 44
Radios, quality of, 42
Railroad station, cleanliness of, 30

Rallies, political, 80, 81
Reading
  learning, 95
  materials, 31, 95
Recreation standards, 153
Re-education
  Cultural Revolution and, 104
  methods, 108
Regimentation, daily, 48
Regional stereotypes, 45
Rent scale, 132
Resources, natural, 137
Respect for elders, 24
Restaurant
  meals, 76, 155
  types of, 57
Restrictions
  on career choice, 120
  on choice, general, 115
  on travel, 115, 181
Revolution, Cultural, 104
Rural. *See also* Commune, Village.
  industrialization, 125
  industries, and local needs, 125
  medicine, 182

S

Safety at night, 82
Salaries, 130
School, schools. *See also* Education.
  choices, lack of, 100
  conditioning, 98
  curriculum, 90
  day, average, 93
  hierarchy, 89
  May 7, purpose of, 108
  ongoing changes in, 112
  practical work in, 90
  special classes, lack in, 100
  system, flaws in, 90
Security, five guarantees of, 215
Segregation by job in housing, 66
Sex education, 211
Sexual practices, 211
Shipyards, importance of, 135
Shopping, problems of, 63, 64
Shops, noodle, 58
Shortages of consumer goods, 63
Shows, open-air, 84
Slavery, custom of, 205
Sleeping accommodations, 42
Slums of Canton, 53

Smoking, popularity of, 172
Snacks
  Chinese, 77
  Western, absence of, 77
Soccer, popularity of, 78
Soldier, Five-Good, 98
Soups, popularity of, 59
Spelling, romanization of, 7
Sports
  on commune, 173
  competition, 79
  facilities, 70
  lack of star system in, 159
  popularity of, 78
  worker-athletes in, 159
Statistics, preoccupation with, 31, 223
Status, work and, 121
Storyteller, public, 195
Strangers, meeting, 68
Street, streets
  of Canton, 48
  committees, 52
Students
  gifted, 113
  labor, 115, 116
  and teachers, relationships of, 89
  university, 101
Sun Yat-sen, work of, 80
Sunday activities, 68
Swimming, popularity of, 79

T

Taching, story of, 144
Talents, developing hidden, 140
Taxes, lack of income, 132
Tea drinking, popularity of, 53
Teacher-student relationships, 89
Teams, commune production, 174
Television
  noncommercial nature of, 159, 160
  as propaganda, 158
  sets, scarcity of, 42
Textile factory, 127
Time, lack of free, 140, 154
Toilets on communes, 170
Tourism, difficulties of, 9
Tours for foreigners, 64
Traditions, use of, 227, 228
Traffic laws, 62
Train
  service, 32
  trip entering China, 27

Transfers, work, 126
Travel restrictions, 115
  effect of, 181
Traveling entertainers, 196

U

United States
  knowledge by people about, 72
  relations with, 12
University, universities
  admission to, 100, 103, 113
  curriculum of, 102
  and factories, relationship of, 109
  performance criteria of, 103, 104
  student body of, 101
Urban
  cleanliness, 48
  crime, 51, 53

V

Vacations, 150
Venereal disease, control of, 213
Village. *See also* Commune, Rural.
  activities, 185
  family, 180
    dinner, 181
  life, 180
    politics in, 184
  rural, appearance of, 179, 180
Visits to China, difficulty in
    arranging, 9, 10

W

Wade-Giles spelling system, 7
Wage, wages
  commune, 189
  scale, 130
Walking
  into China, 30
  popularity of, 60
Weddings, 72
Women. *See also* Girls.
  as barefoot doctors, 216
  contrast to Western, 200
  doctors, Chinese, 218

family role of, 216
feet of, binding, 204
freedom of, 204
in government, 202
household role of, 206
idealization of role of, 203
improvement in status of, 221
labor role of, 202
"liberation" of, 215
marriage relationships of, 207
and men, barriers between, 201
restrictions on, 204
segregation of, 60
support industries of, 124
Work
  advantages, 224
  all ages and, 52
  assignments, 126, 129
  attitude to, 120, 121
  classes after, 147
  commune
    attitude to, 173
    pace of, 166, 171
  community, closeness of, 119
  conditions of, 133
  in country, variety of, 125
  experience, youth, 114, 115
  at home and women, 206
  overtime, 134
  promotions, 135
  respect for, 140
  transfers, 126
Worker, workers
  artists, 148
  as individuals, 118
  ingenuity, 140
  inventions, 140, 141
  and oil industry, 144
  teachers, 145
Writing ideographs, 93

Y

Yang and yin, theory of, 184
Yin and yang, theory of, 184
Youth
  attitude to, 224
  relationships of, 60
  work experience of, 114, 115